COUSINS 2

Also by Selena Haskins

Cousins: All We Got Is Us

A River Moves Forward

Riding the Waves

Poetry from the Colors of My Mind

Yesterday Was a Long Time Ago

Home Is This Way

Just Between Us

She Can Hoop

She Can Dance

COUSINS 2

Family Over Everything

SELENA HASKINS

Hardcover ISBN: 979-8-218-61929-9

First paperback edition 2026

Edited by Emily Michel

Book Formatting: WriteWomenPublish.com

Printed in the USA

For my husband and for my mother;
you are both forever loved and deeply missed.
Not a day goes by when I don't think of you.

Rest in peace,
until we meet again in paradise.

— Love Always,
Selena

Contents

PART I
What Had Happened Was...

ONE

"Lately"

BOOGIE

January 1993

Nicki and I stepped off the train at Benning Road, and I was practically levitating in my heeled boots and a lime-green goose down coat so bright like a highlighter it couldn't be ignored. I just got into Duke Ellington School of the Arts for dance. Even if I got to take two whole trains every day to get there. Darling, it was worth every swipe of that metro card. My heart pounded like bass in a club, and I couldn't stop grinning. Child, I stepped off the escalator and started spinning. Arms stretched wide like I was accepting an award, nearly smacking a passerby with my bookbag.

"I'd like to accept this Tony Award," I announced to absolutely nobody while Nicki laughed and clapped like I already earned a gig in a Broadway show.

The whole DC looked brighter and shinier to me now, like it finally recognized talent when it saw it. I bounced on my toes, as we passed the Shrimp Boat to head to Nicki's place in Simple City. Honey, we were definitely going to celebrate this afternoon over chips and candy bars. *MTV* would be blasting from the TV. And Nicki's living room would be transformed into my first sold-out performance. Because baby, if I had to cross this entire city twice a day from Capitol Hill on two subway trains to chase my dream, best believe I'd do it in style.

"You are going to love Duke, I promise. There are so many talented folks there," Nicki said as we walked up the hill toward her apartment building. Nicki had gotten into Duke when we'd graduated from Hine. She had a beautiful singing voice like Teena Marie.

"I know I will. The whole school will know my name. I'm already hearing the anthem of the TV show *Fame* in my head."

Nicki grinned and said, "Well, you know what Debbie Allen told Leroy, 'Get ready to pay in sweat.' Duke's not just big, it's demanding. But trust me, it's worth it." She'd been at Duke since tenth grade and was now a senior.

I laughed, feeling the excitement bubble up. "Girl, I know it's huge, but I'm ready for whatever comes. Honestly, when I walked in, it reminded me of visiting the White House as a kid, so grand and full of possibilities. I can't wait to dive in!"

"My voice coach told me our auditorium is big so we're ready for larger stages," Nicki said, then blew and popped a big bubble.

"I'm ready for any big stage, honey. I can see it now." I paused my walk, glared up at the sky. "I'll perform at the Lincoln Theater one day, or better yet, have my name in glowing neon lights. Broadway welcomes Boogie Walker and the—"

CRACK.

Something slammed into the back of my head, and the world lit up white. My knees buckled, my ears rang, and the ground turned me loose. Next thing I knew, I was tumbling fast. A crew of thugs about twenty deep with ski coats, hoods low, eyes mean, clobbered me with fists.

"Stop! Leave him alone!" Nicki shouted. They tossed her aside like a freakin' rag doll. Honey, that's when I lost it. It's one thing to come for me, but a whole other thing to hurt my best friend. I stood up, swinging at everything in my way, but I was outnumbered. The fact that I tried to retaliate seemed to piss them off.

One punch felt like it split my lips wide open, and another

plunged into my ribs, knocking the wind out of me. I hit the cold concrete again, but harder.

"Faggot! We told you to stay from around here!" the thugs shouted, as they continued to punch and kick.

I curled into myself, shielding my face from further blows from their boots and fists. Shame, mixed with blood from my nose and mouth, engulfed me. *Please God, make them stop,* I prayed silently to myself. Nicki and I weren't bothering anybody. *God, are you punishing me for what happened to Champ? Please, if you're not punishing me, save me.*

Another voice cut through the commotion. It was calm, firm, but commanding.

"Back off him. Right now."

I peeped through my fingers, as I was still shielding my face. Fear rippled off that pack of thugs. Their tough facades darted to one another, some jaws clenched tight while others hung slack as if unsure whether to run or stay frozen by the guy who commanded them to back off. It was clear his presence rattled them to the core.

"We ain't got no beef with you, Scorpio."

"Then get to steppin."

They quickly walked away as if Scorpio had a gun. Maybe he did, but his voice was enough to make them listen.

Nicki helped me up, but I couldn't stop staring at this guy, Scorpio. I'd heard plenty about him but had never seen him before. He was Turk's cousin from New York, now running things in DC after Turk got locked up. His rep matched his tough image, but he was surprisingly attractive too.

Scorpio stood tall and lean with dark skin that gleamed like polished mahogany. His eyes held a magnetic mystery that drew you in and dared you to look away. Neat, arched brows framed his gaze, and his high-top fade looked fresh from the barber's chair. He rocked a crisp white tee beneath a black Eddie Bauer coat, blue jeans, and Timberland boots so new they looked straight out the box. A crew lingered behind him like shadows, but honey, it was clear he didn't need them. His presence alone was enough to command attention.

"You good, shorty?" Scorpio's voice rolled over me, smooth but deep. For a moment, the ache in my ribs and the sting in my mouth faded into the background. I found myself lost in the force of his bravado.

I winced. "I'm okay…I guess."

Scorpio's gaze shifted to Nicki. "Time to get yourself a new boyfriend. A nigga that's man enough to stand up for you."

"He ain't my boyfriend."

Ouch. Her words came up quick, without a second thought. *Guess I'm spoiled milk?*

Scorpio, with a sly but alluring grin, replied, "If you say so," before moving along with his crew following close behind, making me wish people gave me the same respect.

"Let's get you inside and cleaned up." Nicki took hold of my hand. Not like she did when we were boyfriend and girlfriend at Hine Junior High, but like I was her child who had been wounded. I didn't like it. Not one bit.

Later, in Nicki's room, we watched MTV while she tended to my bruises with Neosporin and Band-Aids, just like her nurse mom would. I pressed an ice pack to my lip and watched Jodeci sing Stevie Wonder's "Lately" as if they were singing to me. Leaning back against the headboard, I was flooded with both shame and embarrassment. Nicki always had my back, but did she really have to tell Scorpio I wasn't her boyfriend like that?

"Does it still hurt?" she asked, clearly thinking about the incident and not my feelings.

I let myself smile, even if it made everything ache. "A little," I answered softly.

"What are you going to tell your mother this time?"

I shrugged. "I'll make something up, like always."

"Boogie, you really need to start defending yourself," she said, frustration in her voice, reminding me of when Champ used to say, *Don't let people pick on you just because you're queer.*

Then I thought about it and asked, "How was I supposed to fight off twenty guys?"

"I'on know." Nicki shrugged.

"Is that why I'm *not* your boyfriend?"

Nicki's brows pinched together. "What are you talking about?"

I looked away for a moment, but the heat of my frustration crawled up my neck. "I didn't like the way you said I wasn't your boyfriend earlier."

"Boogie, don't trip 'cuz you know I didn't mean it like that," she said, taping the last Band-Aid over my brow.

I dropped my chin.

"I'm sorry." She gently rested her hand on top of mine.

"Girl, don't even sweat it." I gave in, not wanting her to think I was being too soft.

"But you *are* special to me." She smiled.

"Really?"

"You were my first boyfriend, and even though I broke up with you, you've always been my best friend. You know all my secrets. That means something."

Feeling grateful, I smiled, leaned in, and kissed her cheek.

She blinked like she was surprised. I'd kissed her cheek before, but that was as far as it ever went. I respected her, but she'd always been a "fast tail girl," per my mom and Grandma. "She's not for you," they would say. Dad, on the other hand, thought she was cute. Nicki *was* cute, but to him, any girl for me would've been.

I felt Nicki's hand against my chin. She turned my head toward her and planted a kiss on my lips. Her lips were soft and without all the fuzz I was used to. When I felt her tongue slither into my mouth, I pulled back. Something inside me felt like this was wrong. I wasn't sure if it was because we were friends or something else.

"Girl, what are you doing?"

She gave me a small shrug. "Kissing you?" Her voice was barely above a whisper, like she felt a little embarrassed by my reaction.

I stared at her, confused. "Nicki, we've been down this road before. You know I'm gay."

And right then, K-Ci hit his famous *Oooo yeahhh* from the TV.

She looked away, cheeks flushed a little red. We sat quietly for a moment, watching K-Ci and JoJo sing until their veins protruded from their necks.

"I know you said you're gay, but if you've never been with a girl before, how do you really know for sure?" She puckered a curious brow.

"It's just a feeling, I guess."

"We've all felt a certain way before, but it doesn't mean we're gay. Like, I think Janet Jackson is beautiful, but that doesn't make me gay."

"Do you think about her sexually, though?"

She twisted her nose. "Ew. No."

"Then maybe that's the difference."

"Nah." She wagged her finger. "See, you haven't been with a girl or a boy. You're just having feelings and thoughts or whatever. As your friend, I think you deserve to know for sure, and there's only one way to find out."

"What are you suggesting?" I propped my hand on my hip, the way Grandma always does.

She took hold of my hand and placed it gently against her boobs. "You can find out with me."

Do it, bro, I imagined Champ saying to me. Memories of the numerous times I'd caught him in action flooded through my mind. Even the one time he almost got caught when my mom came home. He threw that girl into the closet. The poor girl almost suffocated during the night.

"What do you say? It will be our secret," Nicki said, already taking off her clothes. "And if you don't like it, at least you will know for sure, okay?"

"O…K…I…guess so," I gulped.

"I know you're still a little sore, so just lie back and enjoy the ride," she teased.

Nicki climbed on top of me, and a thousand thoughts collided in my mind. Whether I was gay or straight lay somewhere in between me being excited by the poster of George Michael on her wall and loving the softness of how she felt. My hands instinctively had a mind of their own, traveling over her smooth skin. Within minutes, an amazing euphoric sensation shot through me like I couldn't control it if I tried. The incredible feeling made me gasp a moan that I wasn't sure I was supposed, but my pitch was just as high as Nicki's.

My heart pounded, and every muscle relaxed until it all felt weirdly calm. There was this awkward silence that felt way louder than it should have. I stared at the ceiling wondering what would happen next. It felt good and I liked it, but the other part of me felt like I'd betrayed something deeper inside of me.

Nicki was a beautiful girl with long curly black hair, dark lashes, and a body that popped in all the right places. As attractive as she was, I wondered if I was turned on by her or the thought of wanting to *be* her.

I watched as she traced lazy patterns along my stomach and kissed one of the bruised spots so tenderly you would think her lips were going to make it disappear. Her big, pretty eyes looked up at me. "Are you okay?"

I wanted to tell her everything swirling inside of me, but I wasn't sure if I wanted her to unravel my thoughts. All I could say in response was, "I need to get home. It's getting late."

~

A MONTH LATER...

Sunday dinners at Grandma's house were always noisy, with the TV on in the background and family members debating, joking, or laughing out loud. The kitchen smelled of fried chicken and collard greens as kids ran around despite warnings to sit down. Amidst the chaos, my mom asked me to answer the phone just as I was enjoying a piece of Grandma's chicken. Still, there was a certain warmth beneath my family's busy behavior that I always loved. Maybe it was the togetherness.

I paused before taking the next bite. "Ma, all those people in the living room can't hear the phone ringing?" I sighed and stood from the dining room table, brushing crumbs from my USED jeans outfit as I walked into the living room.

"Hello?" I smirked with irritation behind the phone.

Silence.

"HELLO?" I said louder. All I could hear was someone breathing heavy.

"Boogie, it's…it's Nicki."

"Oh… hey, girl. What's up?"

"What do you mean, *what's up*?" she repeated, her voice rising with anger. "Why've you been dodging me at school?"

She wasn't wrong. Ever since we had sex, things between us have felt weird and confusing. I saw my best friend naked, and no matter how hard I tried to unsee it, I couldn't. Sex was supposed to answer the big *what if*, but it didn't.

"Girl, I been so busy with school 'n' stuff." I laughed it off. "You know Duke is new to me, I'm just trying to figure it all out."

"Busy?" she shot back. "Boogie, I know you. Besides dancing with the Rhythm Rock Boys or at school, you're usually at home or you're at your grandma's house, like right now. It's no excuse why you haven't called me back when I've been leaving messages."

I opened my mouth to reply, but then—

"I'm pregnant. That's why I'm calling."

The world stopped spinning on its axis, and my blood froze. The sound of laughter and clinking silverware from the dining room faded to the sound of my pulse thundering in my ears.

"Honey, what?" I hissed.

"You heard me," she sounded more upset. "I took two pregnancy tests and just told my mom. She wants me to see a doctor tomorrow and for you to—"

CLICK.

I hung up before she could finish. My hands trembled as I flipped the ringer switch to off in case she tried to call back. I couldn't have her embarrassing me in front of family.

Lying heifer!

I took a deep breath, composed myself, and returned to the dining room where Lucci was arguing with my great-uncle about the Redskins losing to Dallas again. My younger cousins and Jasmine fought over a toy, and Raven was sitting in the corner reading a *Vogue* magazine with Cindy Crawford on the cover, paying none of us attention.

"Boogie, who was that on the phone?" Mom asked, oblivious to all the commotion, as she passed the iced tea to my dad. They'd been working to rekindle their relationship or whatever.

"Uh... Nicki," I said quickly. "Her cat died."

Mom, with her usual sympathetic demeanor, said, "Oh no, poor thing. Pets can be like family."

Suddenly, my eyes pooled with tears at the thought of Nicki being pregnant.

Jasmine let go of the toy she'd been having a tug of war with, then she noticed my facial expression.

"Don't cry, Boogie. Nicki can get another kitty cat," she said in her innocent five-year-old voice. She was my Boo, and way too young to be an aunt.

Grandma frowned. "Boy, you better wipe them doggone tears. It's just a cat. Nicki can grab another cat from any back alley."

"Oh Mama, don't say it like that," Mom said, tenderly.

"It's the truth. People treat pets better than humans."

The table continued in chatter. I forced a smile and poked at my plate, but honey, my appetite was gone. I was barely eighteen and hadn't graduated from high school yet. The thought of being a father scared me. Where was Leslie when I needed her?

TWO

A Long Way from Home

LESLIE

February 16, 1993

Dear Diary,

It's been a while since I wrote, but tonight I had an unexpected call from Boogie that left me stunned. He told me he got his best friend, Nicki, pregnant. We'd always assumed he was gay, so this news is hard for all of us to process. Although it's been difficult to stay in touch with family with so much schoolwork, I was glad I was able to take the call from Boogie. I missed my little cousin-brother. I didn't see any of my family over the winter holiday break because of my other plans. I'd saved my money to fly out to San Diego to visit Mitch. He'd been traveling to New York since my freshman year, so I thought I'd surprise him and fly out West. He was pleasantly surprised! We had an amazing time. Mitch hopes to be stationed closer to home soon, and I can't wait.

As Johnny Gill's singing "Long Way from Home" on my radio, it's making me think about how much my cousins' lives are changing. Raven is a freshman at Howard. She wants to be a television news anchor and said she'd like to pledge Alpha Kappa Alpha like her mom. She may already be a Soror since I haven't spoken to her in over a month. Lucci's caught up in baby mama drama per his last letter to me, and now Boogie is about to be a father too? Wow!

Meanwhile, I've been busy too with studying and writing papers, and trying to find another internship with a newspaper. Until then, I'm working night shifts at Butler Library, which I prefer over working at the cafeteria like I did when I was a freshman, where I packed on the pounds I didn't need. I ate a lot because I missed home.

I miss Grandma's cooking, and Mama, though she still isn't talking, I miss seeing her face. I wonder if she's forgotten about me.

Anyway, I need to head out. Speaking of work, I have a shift tonight and plan to stop by Junior's for cheesecake and coffee beforehand.

Until next time,

Leslie

THREE

Living In Silence

IRENE WALKER

People saw me as strange, but my mind was crowded with unspoken words. Anxiety held me back from talking, so I followed my hospital routine: got my pills, showed the nurse, moved along. The nurse was polite but distant. Sometimes, I saw a mischievous little girl in a red dress. It was my hallucination trying to cause trouble, making me quietly laugh. In therapy, Ms. Lanham encouraged me to draw to explain these visions and my feelings. She suggested the girl represents my childhood wounds and a longing for self-expression. Maybe she was right. When the girl disappeared, I still wondered if she was the last innocent part of me.

"Keep going to the common room," said one of the security officers in charge of hallway monitoring. He pointed further down the hall, as if I was a schoolgirl who needed direction. I'd been here for three years; he acted like I didn't know where to go. Last I checked, I was a forty-one-year-old grown woman.

As I walked toward the common room, my thoughts continued to twist and flicker around in my mind. Images of Mama's face the night I attacked her for slapping Leslie flashed behind my eyes. Her mouth yelled at me, my hand rose, I struck her, and she flipped backward, cigarette hitting the curtains, and then the sudden bloom of fire swallowed everything in the bathroom and upstairs.

The sound of a little child crying made me look over my shoulder. It wasn't the little girl in the red dress but the black one. She was sitting on the floor in the hallway.

"She represents the guilt you feel," Ms. Lanham had told me when I had mentioned in writing that I always saw her when I felt bad about something.

I wanted to go to the little girl, to whisper that it was okay, that we didn't mean to hurt anyone. But the guards urged us to move along. I never wanted to hurt my mother. God knows that. But guilt had teeth that gnawed at me sometimes.

The Jenny Jones Show was playing on the TV when I walked into the common room. It was an episode that seemed to be about imposters and liars. I looked away. Lord knows I've had my share of betrayers and imposters, starting with my sister, Diane. She's the reason I'm here and why my brother Donovan is in prison. And then there was Percy Knight, the monster who took my voice and left me hollow. So, no, I didn't need to watch anything that reminded me of cruel people.

Patients shuffled past me as I sat down in my usual seat by the window. Each one of them was trapped in their own storm too. Some talked to themselves and laughed at nothing. Some, like me, said nothing at all. I heard plenty of stories here, even though I can't talk, I listen well. And I've come to realize that most of us didn't end up here because we were crazy or dangerous. We're here because someone else was.

Only good thing about this place was this room, where the sunlight slipped through the barred windows and caught the dust, making it drift like lost prayers.

And speaking of prayers, Mama never stopped. She told the psychiatrists, "We're praying she comes out of this." The doctors diagnosed me with schizophrenia, PTSD, and selective mutism.

"In time," they told Mama, "she may speak again, once her mind reconnects with reality."

I didn't like reality. Not after Percy Knight raped me. Sometimes, I can still feel his hands tightening around my throat at night when I go to sleep. Still hear him whisper against my ear, *"If you tell anyone, I'll kill you."* I was scared that he would. Something snapped inside of me, and I got him before he could get me or hurt someone else again. I'm not evil. I wasn't crazy, nor was I the "window witch" the neighborhood kids called me. I got a name. I was Irene Walker, and God loved me and saw me even when people didn't.

An orderly approached. "Irene, you got a visitor."

I jumped up eagerly from the chair, grinning as I followed him down the hallway toward the visitors' room. The two little girls walked in front of me now, holding hands and skipping along. I took a couple of hard blinks, and they disappeared. Meds must have started to work now.

As soon as I walked in, I spotted Mama amongst the crowd of patients and guests. She sat behind a wooden table in her peach floral spring dress, reminding me that winter had come and gone. Slowly, I took a seat across from her. Guards hovered nearby, ready to pounce if anyone in the room lost control. I never did. But that didn't stop them from watching us.

The table between my mother and me bore names carved by other patients who probably sought proof of their existence. I traced my fingers over their names as Mama started having small talk about the goings-on back home.

"… and Leslie's doing well," Mama said, eyes softening behind her bifocals. That was when I looked up. What hurt most was being absent from my daughter's life, unable to give advice or share experiences like other mothers.

"She made the dean's list again, too," Mama continued. "She found a newspaper internship and won't be home for spring break. She's also visiting Mitch in Norfolk. Said he's looking for a place to live since the Navy stationed him there now. She must really be in love, since she's prioritizing him over family. I just love the two of them together, but I sure do miss her."

Love? I hope she's careful of that. My heart skipped nervously.

"At least she's got just one more year at Columbia before she comes home for good," she said with a nervous grin.

My mouth parted. I wanted to say something so bad, but it just wouldn't come out. Then I saw that one of the guards had left his clipboard with a notepad at the edge of the table. My fingers twitched, hesitating. *What if Mama thinks I may harm her with the pen? Shut up. Shut up. Bad thoughts. Focus on the good.*

The urge to communicate won over as I talked myself through it. Slowly, I reached for the pen and pad. Mama's eyes followed and expanded on my every move. Her breath caught. She watched as if she was excited and afraid of what I was about to do. I grabbed the clipboard when the guard walked away, his attention drawn by a lady having a manic moment. A mix of wonder and fear danced across Mama's face.

I pressed the pen to the paper like I'd always done in therapy, but for some reason I felt so nervous in front of Mama. *Come on. Write. Please. Say it. You can do it.* The letters came out shaky and uneven.

I wrote:

I am proud of Leslie. I miss her so much.

Mama's eyes glistened as she read each word. Her hand trembled to her mouth. For the first time in forever, she looked like she believed in me again as her cheeky smile blushed rosily.

"Irene… you can write?" Her voice cracked on my name.

I nodded, barely. *Don't get too excited now. Don't make me more nervous, Mama. I don't like attention.*

Tears spilled down her cheeks. "Oh, my God. Thank you!" She lifted her eyes heavenward. "This—this is wonderful. I'll tell Leslie and—"

"Give me that!" One of the guards came from nowhere, snatched the clipboard and pen from in front of me. I dropped my chin. Embarrassed. Watched the little girl in the black dress appear and then she ran off crying and screaming that she was sorry. I crawled back into my shell.

"You don't have to be that way with her," Mama snapped, rolling her eyes as the guard walked away without a care, clipboard and pen in hand. "Don't let him get to you, Irene. If you want to write more, I will bring you some paper and pens next time, you hear?"

I lifted my eyes slowly. Tried to smile to assure her that I was okay.

"I didn't mean to be so loud, but I can't wait to tell Leslie and—"

I shook my head no rapidly. I wasn't ready to be put on the spot. Not right now. Not yet. That's when Mama reached across the table and covered my hand with hers. Her palm felt warm and motherly.

"I understand. When you're ready," she nodded gently. "But this is good progress."

In her eyes I could see there was no fear or worry anymore. It was faith and love. When she finally stood up to leave, she didn't rush. She walked around the table, wrapped her arms around me, and whispered, "I love you, Irene. Always have and I always will."

I wanted to say it back, but I couldn't. The desire to communicate any further was gone. Gone to the mean guard who walked away with the tools for me to do so.

I stared at the empty chair after Mama left. The loneliness instantly returned. I felt like I was slipping back into my own world.

"This is yours." The guard walked back over to me, ripping the page I'd written on. I looked at it.

I am proud of Leslie. I miss her so much. I wrote crookedly only because I was nervous. Still, it was my honest expression, the way I'd learned to write in therapy. When I looked up, the little girl in the red dress kicked the guard in the butt! And I giggled under my breath. A light came back on inside of me. Perhaps this was a new beginning soon to come…

FOUR

Trapped

LUCCI

G-Ma was visiting Aunt Irene at St. Elizabeth's, so the whole house was mine for a couple of hours. My spot was the basement, my musical kingdom since the fire. Insurance came through and redid the whole crib from top to bottom. Fresh drywall, new floors, and the whole shebang!

Spring fever was in full effect, as me and Tasha was working up a sweat while Intro was singing "Come Inside." Legs bent over my shoulder. Nails dug into my flesh. Sweat spilled down my back as she moaned my name. Sending a brother's ego shooting to the moon.

"Lucci, stop." Tasha pushed my shoulders back.

I panicked, stopped right away. I didn't think I was hurting her but pleasing her.

"Wha-wha-what's wrong?"

"I think I heard something from upstairs."

I tried to listen over the music playing in the background but didn't hear anything.

"Nah, it's just us. Nobody's here," I continued, trying to get mine.

"Mmm, I don't know… maybe we should stop," she pushed again.

"Oh, come on Tasha, it's nothing. Let's finish up."

Suddenly, the basement door screeched open.

"Lucci, are you down there?"

Shoot. That's Boogie. Why did G-Ma have to give him a key?

We panicked and scrambled for our clothes. Tasha hopped on one leg, trying to pull up her skirt while I grabbed a T-shirt and shorts.

"Hold on, Cuz! Got company!" I yelled, still half-dressed. Tossed the condom in the trash. I hurried to the bathroom and washed my hands. When I heard Boogie walking down the steps, I thought this dude was impatient or just being nosy.

Soon as his kicks hit the floor, Boogie hit me with that look. His eyebrows high, judgment on deck, like *what the hell is going on.* His big brown eyes flicked from me to Tasha.

I cleared my throat. "Uh, Boog, this Tasha. Tasha, this my cousin Boogie."

She barely said a "hey" before snatching her purse from the chair in the corner. "I thought you said this was your personal space."

"It is. Boogie is just visiting. Don't trip. He won't be here long."

"Some other time, Lucci. I gotta go."

And just like that, all that big booty jiggled up the stairs, and my good time went out the door with it.

I turned around sharply to Boogie. "Man, you just killed my whole vibe!"

He pinched his nose. "Whatever! It smells like the Wharf down here. Tasha needs a Massengill or something. And you better go to the clinic after banging a stinky chick like that."

"I stay strapped now, bro, trust."

"I hope so." He grabbed the Glade off the shelf and started sprayin' like a mad pest control man. "How old is Tasha, anyway? She looks old enough to be your mother."

"She said she's twenty-three. I lied and told her I was twenty-one just so I could hit that."

He clucked his tongue as he said, "Lies been told, honey, cuz she looks like she ain't seen twenty-three since rotary phones. And that big-haired weave job died in '85."

"Don't matter to me."

"Just sayin'." He quietly eased down in a chair, crossed his legs in his usual dramatic fashion.

"So, what's up with you, man? Sound off," I said, while I flipped the sofa bed back into the couch.

He hesitated at first and then poured out about Nicki *again.* You know, the pregnancy, the jokes at school, his parents wildin' cuz they thought he was gay but got a girl pregnant, and now the Rhythm Rock Boys, his dance crew, may be replacing him. The young buck was spiraling downhill. When he finished, my head felt dizzy.

I sat down on the sofa, fired up a blunt. "Welcome to my world."

He groaned. "I didn't sign up for this mess."

"You think I did?" I retorted. "Anyway, let me ask you something, man, how you end up with Nicki in the first place? Thought y'all were best friends, and I thought you were gay. No offense."

"None taken. Call it curiosity, and this cat has been killed."

I laughed. "Well, man-to-man, cousin-to-cousin, did you like it?"

He shrugged. "I did, but ask me if it was worth this trouble and I'd say no."

"I can dig it," I puffed, then exhaled. "Well, when is the baby due?"

"November? I think. Gotta find me a job. This is...this is a nightmare, Cuz. Can't believe it." He started getting choked up and covered his face with both hands.

"Come on, Boog, Walker men don't do that crying stuff. We rise, know what I'm saying?"

He wiped his eyes. "But I'm not ready to be a father. I can't do this."

I got up and gave Cuz some love. Hugged him and said, "Everything gonna be alright, Cuz."

I turned him loose, let him stew in it for a sec while I walked over to my little studio in the corner. I fired everything up: amps, keyboard, drum machine, and the speakers that buzzed to life. I stepped over the wires scattered across the floor like vines and slipped into my makeshift booth. Naughty by Nature, Scarface, and LL Cool J stared down from the posters on the walls, daring me to level up. The beat kicked in with the bass so heavy it rattled my bootcamp trophies from Ohio. Next to them were pictures of my boys, Donovan and Lil Lucci. One look at my shorties and the words started bubbling up inside of me. I let the beat pull them out of me.

Two smiles, same teeth, with different shades,
Donovan's honey brown, like sun-soaked braids.
Lil Lucci light-skinned, with them almond eyes,
His mama Asian but acts Black, and she's fly.
She named our son Lucci
Thought it was my real name
But my girl Keisha gave my other son my government name
Two kids, two mamas, my soul's under pressure,
Tryna keep it balanced, but life don't measure.
Keisha was my Black queen, strong on my side,
cheated with Ling, who was my chick on the side.
Knocked them both up, two sons the same age.
Can a brother borrow some loot so the bills can get paid?
I'm trapped. Like a mouse with no way out.
Tryna make a living get out my grandma house.
I'm trapped…

"I hear you over there, Cuz." Boogie perked up.

"That sound alright?"

"Yeah, keep going."

I feel trapped,
Like a mouse with no way out,
Tryna get a deal and get out my grandma's house.
Two baby mamas bringin' drama,
Shoulda wrapped it up, shoulda wore a condom.
Tryna stay off the block, can't get shot,

don't want a joker to rob what little I got…

The phone started ringing on the nightstand, interrupting my flow. I set the headset down. Boogie beat me to it when he answered it.

"It's Keisha." He handed me the cordless phone.

"Yo, you on the mic, what's your beef?" I answered.

"LUCCI!" Keisha's voice exploded. "Donovan's daycare called. You still haven't paid the bill, and now she's saying he can't come back!"

Oh, snap! Forgot all about that joint.

She kept going. "Your grandmother needs to watch him tomorrow cuz I'm completely booked at the shop with Easter being this weekend."

I couldn't even tell her I spent the money on a new recording system. Circuit City had that sale, so I had to cop it.

Boogie was laughing as he overheard her. Probably thought my drama eased his.

Keisha was still buggin' out in my ear, so I turned the beat back up and freestyled over her:

Bills due, baby cryin', confusion on the rise,
Money short, time gone, no alibis.
One call, one moment, it all goes sideways,
Tryna keep my rhythm while she playin' the hard way…

"Lucci, are you even listening to me?" Keisha shouted.

"Yo, Boog, write that verse down for me."

"So you just gon' ignore me?"

"Don't trip, a'ight? I got you. I'll get the money next week," I told her, then hung up. I stepped back into the booth, grabbed the mic:

Gotta stay sharp, gotta move fast,
Life don't wait, and money don't last.
One foot in a dope beat, one foot in a mess,

but I'm Lucci Loot, I don't survive, I finesse.

Boogie clapped. "Now *that* is hot!"

I put my headphones down on the music stand. "For real young?"

"Honey, yes! You gotta record that ASAP!"

"It's called 'Trapped.' Just need to put it all together," I said, taking the paper from Boogie. I jotted down the next verse.

"You know, you should perform that song tonight at Tracks for teen night. The crowd'll love it!"

"That ain't my scene, but you go own that stage. Go make those Rhythm Rock Boys reconsider, Cuz!"

We dapped up. He bounced, and I turned the music back up. If this rap music don't save me, nothing will.

FIVE

Glitter and Neon Lights

RAVEN

The bass was booming under my heels the second we walked into Tracks Night Club for teens' night. The walls were literally flashing these crazy electric pink and blue colors, and the whole place smelled like perfume, heat, and total freedom. The crowd was already packed with, you know, a bunch of queer teens just dancing and vibing, like they were totally trying to prove something. It was as if being "happy" meant rebellion against society's normal, and confidence meant flaunting sequins and glitter in drag as armor.

Crystal Waters's classic hit "Gypsy Woman (She's Homeless)" spilled from the speakers as my sorority sisters and I sat near the stage. I wore vintage Versace pants, high heels, and matching earrings with my silk top—my style earned me the nickname Glam-Girl amongst my Sorors. But tonight, the focus wasn't on my look or accessories; it was all about supporting my cousin Boogie.

"This place is wild!" Tierra shouted over Crystal Waters singing *la-da-di-lah-da-dah.*

"I second that," Camille said, clinking her glass to Tierra's. They were legally old enough to drink, I wasn't yet. Just nineteen, but they always figured out a way to get me into clubs even if it wasn't teen night.

"Girls, welcome to Tracks, where glitter and neon lights *are* the culture." I smiled.

We nibbled on hot wings and gossiped while admiring the fabulous, extravagant outfits all around us. A fashion show took place, followed by a few performances of singing, comedy, and even a small funny skit.

"My cousin's about to shut. This place. Down," I said with emphasis, excitement rising in my chest. "Watch."

The MC's voice boomed over the speakers to announce the next act. "Give it up for the *Rhythm Rock Boys!*"

The crowd erupted as if they had been waiting all night long for this part of the show. The opening bass of "Follow Me" by Aly-Us filled the room. Boogie stepped onto the stage with his crew, shimmering in silver dance gear that hugged every muscle. The crowd was instantly transfixed, dancing and clapping along, standing up in the chairs. Super hyped!

Their choreography started smoothly, then snapped into overdrive, bodies slicing the air with precision. Then Boogie took center stage. He wasn't just dancing, he was *commanding.* His spins, his dips, those crisp arm movements with each one hitting like punctuation. You could literally *feel* him.

Camille leaned in, grinning. "Girl, Boogie is doing the thang! You hear me? I can see why you're his biggest fan, but I've become one of them tonight, trust."

"Of course," I said. "My cousin was voguing way before Madonna turned it mainstream."

"Honey, he doesn't even need backup," Tierra added. "He's a one-man show."

"Been telling him that since he was at Hine Junior High," I replied, wiping my mouth after stealing the last hot wing.

The crowd lost their minds as Boogie nailed every beat. Then, in one electric moment, he flipped backward and landed in a perfect split under the golden lights. The place erupted!

Boogie had owned that stage and earned a standing ovation. That is, if you weren't already standing and cheering.

After the show, I pushed through a crowd of fans to find him backstage, drenched in sweat but glowing.

"Boogie!" I called. He turned around after snapping a picture with two tall drag queens. "You were insane, Boo Boo!"

"Did you see my split at the end?"

"See? Baby, I *witnessed.* I need a therapist just to unpack how proud I am of you."

He giggled, wrapping me in a hug. "I was so nervous!"

"Didn't show," I said. "You lit that stage on fire. The Rhythm Rock Boys were just extras."

"I showed them!"

"Yes, you did! That's why they left here so fast. They were just jealous of all the love people showed you tonight."

"When you said you'd come, I felt you out there," he said, wiping his face with a towel. "You made me wanna give it my all."

"You'll never have to look too far to find me," I told him. "I'll be the loud one throwing roses from the front-row seats."

"Love you, doll baby." He kissed my cheek.

"Love you too."

"I gotta get home. You know Mayor Pratt started that new curfew for teens seventeen and under," he said.

"Too bad. The girls and I are going to grab something to eat at IHOP."

"Well, have fun. Catch you next time," he said, quickly turning away to snap a picture with an admiring fan.

THE GIRLS and I were shoulder-to-shoulder in a cramped IHOP booth, half-tipsy, half-starved, laughing over oversized plates of waffles and omelets. The whole place was filled with clubgoers chasing their midnight hunger. We were talking about summer plans since we only had a month of school left, when Camille threw her hands up dramatically.

"Okay, but can we talk about how iconic your cousin Boogie's show was tonight?"

"Boogie danced circles around everybody," Tierra mumbled through a mouthful of waffle.

"You mean the way he twirled like a Slinky? Girl, it was like he didn't have bones." Camille chimed in.

I laughed, feeling warmth bubbling in my chest with pride for Boogie. "He was amazing. Too bad he couldn't come with us because of that curfew."

"Sometimes I forget he won't be eighteen until this summer," Tierra said.

I lifted my glass of OJ. "I know, right? Anyway, cheers to my cuzzo, Boogie!"

"To Boogie!" they echoed back.

My girls started talking about our sorority car wash coming up, but I couldn't stop thinking about Boogie. I can't believe my cousin's about to be a dad! He's the same boy who danced across Grams's floor in tube socks. Now Nicki turns up pregnant during his big glow-up? Does she think he has money or what? I find it odd she always resurfaces after his talent show earnings.

Tierra snapped her fingers in front of my face. "Rave. Your beeper is vibrating."

Camille smirked. "Ten bucks says it's your baller boo."

I picked it up off the table. Dawson's number lit up the screen, soft green glow washing over me, and making my stomach flutter. He was my babe. That is, whenever he acted right and I didn't catch him cheating on me.

"Bets are off. It's him." I winked, sliding out of the booth and stepping outside to call him back on the payphone.

The warm spring night wrapped around me, reminding me that summer was on the way. I pressed the phone to my ear. Dawson's voice came through deep, sexy, and familiar.

"… and I called your place, but your roommate said you were still out. Figured I'd page you. Find out where you were," he was saying, as if he was worried about my whereabouts. *So sweet!*

"We came to IHOP after Boogie's show tonight."

"Cool. I'm sure he nailed it."

"He sure did."

"I won't keep you long from your girls, but I wanted to let you know I talked to Coach."

My heart perked up. "What'd he say?"

"He thinks my chances of getting drafted to the NBA might be better if I play overseas in Italy. Starting this summer after graduation."

The parking lot felt like it tilted. "Wait…*overseas*? Italy?"

He laughed, slow and smooth. "Yeah, crazy, right? He's even got prospects for me."

"That's not exactly what I was expecting you to say, but—"

"What? You aren't happy?"

He said it like this was good news for both of us. As if he didn't see the way the word *overseas* sliced me open.

"What about…us?" My voice cracked before I could stop it. "I mean, I'm happy for you, I guess." I swallowed hard. I had news of my own to share, but not tonight.

"Rave, I know you're worried."

"Well, yeah," I said softly, switching the phone to my opposite ear as strangers walked by.

"Try to see the big picture. This is my future we're talking about here."

His future. Not ours nor the…never mind.

I blinked fast, but the tears still gathered, stinging my eyes. I never let myself think about losing him. Even when girls were lined up after games, smiling too hard, wearing too little. Even when rumors floated around about him cheating. I held on. I believed in him. Loved him enough to ignore each time I found lace panties in his bed that weren't mine. I forgave him repeatedly, and we were right back together easily. And now he was asking me to "see the big picture" when all I could see was the space he was about to leave behind and me holding the bags while he had a grand ole time overseas.

"I gotta go, there's a pizza delivery at the door," Dawson sounded hurried.

"At this hour?"

"Don't trip babe. I'm hungry."

"Okay…love you," I chased.

"Yep. Love you too. Bye."

CLICK

He hung up too quickly. I can bet my last dollar that some girl was delivering the pizza.

The queasy feeling in my stomach returned, and I doubled over, retching again on the asphalt of the parking lot.

A passing stranger slowed and asked, "Hey, are you okay?"

I waved him off. "It's fine."

Even though nothing felt fine. Suddenly, it was like my entire world was coming apart at the seams. Deep down, I already knew what my heart refused to admit. Dawson would be overseas, and we'd be separated for months. All the fun we'd shared would be behind us, and I couldn't help but wonder what reasons he'd give for unanswered calls from thousands of miles away. Would he find another party or someone else to chase? Or maybe, while he was gone, I'd be forced to face that he left me behind, quietly carrying something I never expected, something far bigger than just loneliness.

I needed Leslie. She always knew what to say. But she was in New York, probably surrounded by books for some Columbia research marathon. I miss her. I could still see us on Grams's front porch and her telling me when my boyfriend Taj and I used to have issues in high school, "Don't ever lose yourself over some guy, Rave." What if I already had?

The door to the IHOP swung open. Tierra and Camille stepped out. I tried to play it off as I stood up and wiped my mouth.

"Are you okay?" Tierra asked, her eyes widening with concern.

"You left us with the bill like you ran off to join witness protection," Camille laughed, half-drunk.

"Sorry. I'll cover dinner tomorrow."

Tierra tilted her head. "Is Dawson okay?"

"Yeah," I murmured as we walked to her car. "He's good." *I'm not.*

"Were you, like, upchucking?" Camille asked, looking back at me from the front passenger seat.

"Must've been those eggs," I lied. IHOP never missed a beat when it came to food.

"Pepto will be the winner. Got some in my dorm room. Swing by," Camille said.

I leaned back against the seat, stared at the moon disappearing behind a sheet of clouds, feeling like I was watching my dreams of being with Dawson disappear too.

SIX

Home Feels Far Away

LESLIE

The city's glow spilled through my dorm window, painting my tower of textbooks like an academic shrine. My desk was a mess of open notebooks, empty coffee cups, and toppled highlighters. Finals had fried my brain! While I'm grateful Columbia lets me chase my journalism dream, I still have to survive this last stretch of junior year. After months of cold walks, overpriced lattes, and New York's chaos, my heart was ready to be in Norfolk with Mitch.

I can't help but smile whenever I think of him and remember his steady voice, his easy laugh, and how he always calls me his peace. I'm so proud that he's applying to become an electrician's mate, and he still has another year serving in the Navy. For now, he's picking up a temp job in Norfolk, just waiting for that acceptance letter. When I was home for spring break, I helped him to find a cozy condo by the water, and now he's turning it into his own little piece of heaven. Even with all the craziness of junior year and my journalism deadlines, knowing he's building a good future, makes me feel assured about what lies ahead for us.

"You're going to love it, Les. Can't wait for our morning pier walks, seafood on the docks, and long nights together," he'd teased when we last talked. Home wasn't a place right now, it was Mitch.

The phone jolted me out of my reverie. *Howard University,* the Caller ID read—2:05 a.m. It had to be Raven. I pictured her returning to her dorm from a nightclub or party, heels clicking, lip gloss shining, hair styled high and flawless. Her world was brunches and sorority mixers. Mine is caffeine and deadlines. She was the social butterfly; I burned the midnight oil in academic pursuits. Still, I smiled when I answered because she's family, and I was glad to hear from her.

"Hello?"

"Les?" she whispered like she was hiding in a closet. "You're up?"

"Got no choice. Girl, these finals are trying to assassinate me."

"I just needed to hear a familiar voice."

I sat up straight. "What did Dawson do this time?"

"He's leaving this summer to play ball overseas."

"That's huge!" I said aloud. *And now he'll have an international buffet of girls.*

"I'm happy for him, I guess. It's just that everything's changing. I'm not sure I'm ready for all of this. We've been together for like ten months, but it feels like forever, you know."

"Counting the times you broke up, I thought it would feel short."

She scoffed. "Hah, hah, hah. You got jokes?" Then she said in a softer more vulnerable tone. "I just don't want him to go, but I also don't want him to think I'm trying to trap him or hold him hostage from his dream."

"Change isn't bad. Just inconvenient sometimes."

She sighed, then skipped the subject. "So, are you coming home after finals?"

"Actually, I'm going to Norfolk first. Mitch and I already made plans."

"Oh." The drop in her tone was impossible to miss. She sounded wounded. "I was hoping we'd spend some time together, but you're always with Mitch during breaks."

My chest tightened a little. She wasn't wrong. I *had* spent the last two breaks wrapped up in Mitch's arms instead of balancing it with family. But love demanded priority, didn't it?

"We'll catch up," I promised. "Soon."

"Feels like we're in two different worlds."

I really didn't know what to say. Gone were the days of hanging outside laughing while cicadas made loud mating noises, and the boys hooped at Watkins playground or played football in the middle of the street.

"I miss us, Les. I hope you really come home after your visit with Mitch this time," Raven finally said, breaking the moment of silence.

"I miss you too. I'll call when I get back to DC and we'll go shopping."

After we said goodbye, I caught my reflection in the window. My eyes looked as exhausted as I felt. Still, there was a spark left in me to finish my paper before morning. Outside, New York glowed with its usual bright lights and wild energy. I've grown to love the city's fiery spirit. It challenged and shaped me the way Columbia had. I'm prepared for the reality of becoming a journalist. But Raven was right, I hadn't been home in a while, and family was feeling too far away from my heart.

SEVEN

Pink Slip Blues

LUCCI

My alarm blasted at 4:30 like it wanted to fight. I'd been up late laying down tracks, so I stayed in bed a minute, wishing I was on stage instead of having to get up to be Lucci the trashman. Within a few minutes, I showered up, put on my green uniform with the neon vest brighter than my future, and laced up my boots. Headed upstairs, following the aroma of bacon. My stomach was growling like a mug.

"Morning, baby," G-Ma said, handing me a big plate of breakfast like I was a king about to battle. "Eat somethin'. You got a long day ahead, and so do I."

"Appreciate you, G-Ma," I mumbled, half-awake. "Thanks for watchin' little Donovan. I'll pay you back. Promise."

"Mm-hmm." She pursed her lips and walked into the living room where Donovan lay on the couch asleep. She didn't buy my promise for a second. Can't blame her. I made too many and broke them all.

BY SIX, I was already at the yard. Diesel blew in the air as trucks rumbled. I was rapping with the old heads. We had coffee mugs in our hands, and the energy was live like an episode of *Sanford & Son*. Me? I was like that dude Lamont, youngest kid tryna survive their jokes and life lessons. Sometimes I'd spit some rhymes from my songs, and they'd give me feedback.

"Donovan! Come here!" Mr. Kenny yelled. He only used my government name when I messed up, and you best believe I used to mess up plenty. No idea why he wanted to see me now.

"Yo, I'll be right back," I told the fellas, and headed over to the office trailer.

Mr. Kenny was a man of few words, but I like how positive he could be at times. When trucks broke down, or weather was a pain, he'd say, "Nothing a pair of jumper cables can't fix," or "Drive slow in the snow. Let's stay safe, even if we're late."

But today? The minute he shut the door behind me, I thought to myself, *something ain't right.*

The TV on Mr. Kenny's desk played the local news until he shut it off and sat down. Behind him hung his most prized possession. It was a Giants jersey signed by Lawrence Taylor. He usually only talked about sports. Since it's basketball playoffs right now, I'd thought about asking if the Bulls could win another chip but today wasn't for small talk. He looked up at me, and the way his thick eyebrows knotted, I thought they were ready to fight.

"The city cut our contract," he said flat. "Had to let some go. You're one of them. Sorry, son."

My stomach dropped. Knees felt weak. "Man, are you serious?"

"Wish I wasn't."

My hands balled into fists in my pockets. "But I'm barely gettin' by as it is. Ling got me paying child support, and I'on know how much longer G-Ma can handle Donovan."

"You're young. You'll bounce back."

"Bounce back from what? Everybody love sayin' that when it's not them fallin'."

"Trust me, we all fall down sometimes, kid," he said, then slid an envelope across the desk. "That's a little somethin' for your boys, but don't tell a soul I gave it to you."

I open the envelope, thumb through it—*three hunnid.* Gonna be gone in a week.

"Thanks," I muttered, pride still stinging like a jab.

"You been a solid young man lately. I respect that. Your last check will be in the mail."

"Yeah, alright man," I mumbled, tucking the envelope in my back pocket.

His eyes softened, and a small smile appeared. "You got talent with that rappin' stuff. Don't let this stop you."

I grinned slightly, surprised he noticed.

"I'll put your platinum record next to the jersey one day."

A smile broke through. "You think I'm that good?" I asked.

"Would I lie?"

"Nah. Thanks, Mr. Kenny. Means a lot coming from you."

We shook hands.

"Go out there and be great, son. Make us all proud."

When I left the yard, I knew I couldn't go home yet. Wasn't ready emotionally to face G-Ma, so I rode around watching the city open up.

By noon, I was starving. Bought some wings with mumbo sauce and fries from 15th Street carryout by Payne Elementary School. That's when Marlo popped out of the barbershop next door. Couldn't miss him. He was tall and skinny, neck so long he could box a giraffe. We used to live in Cappers together.

"Sup, Lucci," he said. We dabbed up and joined the block boys hanging out on the corner. You know, the dealers from Kentucky Courts and Potomac Gardens, thieves, ex-cons, or just honest cats needing that corner therapy, know what I'm saying? It was like twenty dudes deep out that piece.

Before word spread I got cut loose, I drove to East Capitol Street to tell Ling and Keisha myself. Their nail and hair salons were on the same side of the street.

I took a deep breath, feeling like I was about to walk into the lion's den. I opened the door and entered Ling's family-owned business, Polished & Pretty nail salon. The place was all the way live like a beehive on Jolt Cola, but there she was, Ling, filing some chick's nails. She looked like she was auditioning for TLC in her denim and neon outfit. Her hair was styled in braids, and she wore a matching neon cap tilted to the side, the whole vibe like she was Left-Eye.

The door chimed behind me, announcing my doom, and she looked up. I swear for a second, her face went from "Hey, can I help you?" to "Oh no, he didn't just walk up in here like we cool." Her slanted eyes softened for half a second like she might smile… then BAM—they locked onto me with enough venom to spit fire. She stopped filing mid-stroke, like she just remembered she left the stove on at home and marched straight at me.

"Where me money at?" she snapped.

I froze, rubbed the back of my neck, thought to myself, *probably should've just called.*

"Got laid off this mornin', but I'ma get it to you soon as I get my last check."

She shook her head in disbelief. "Eh? You say that two month ago."

Ling was so loud that customers turned to see what was going on. Next thing I knew, her Pops, Mr. Wong, came from the back office. Took one look at me and started cursing me out. Thought he was about to do karate on me or something.

"…and you, no good for grandson. And you, no good for daughter either." Mr. Wong pointed as he spoke each word like he was typing them into the air.

"But I—"

He waved, cuttin me off. "Leave now. You no come back again," Mr. Wong said like I was a stray dog.

When I turned around to leave, the door swung open. Little Lucci came in with another dude holding an ice cream cone. His eyes lit up at the sight of me.

"Dad-dee!"

"Hey son," I leaned down, invited him into my arms when suddenly, the guy with him snatched him up to keep him from running to me.

"He ain't your daddy no more," the guy sneered with a frown. He had an ugly face that only a mother could love, filled with scars like he'd been in a few fights.

"Slim, you better gimme my son!" I was heated. Ready to add another lump to his face.

"Your son? I'm more of his daddy than you are." He wiped the ice cream from Lucci's mouth.

"Ling, who is this? You just gonna let him claim my son?"

"You heard my Pa, get out now. Go! Get out!" Ling shouted like it was final.

Little Lucci started crying. I tried to pick him up.

"Step off!" The dude shoved me back with his free hand, held Lucci in the other like he was his prize and I lost.

I shoved him back. Stared him down. I told him through clenched teeth, "Touch me again and see what happens!"

"You don't want none of this, trust me." He exposed the gun he had at the front of his shorts.

"Easy, Rob. No violence," Mr. Wong said to him, then turned to me. "Please, Lucci, just go. We don't want more trouble."

Ling grabbed the phone, probably calling the cops, so I dipped. Keisha could wait.

BACK ON 15TH, I parked by Payne Elementary. My heart felt heavy seeing my son cry like that. Stress sat on me like it paid rent. Soon as I walked across the street to the corner, the homies took one look at me and went in the carryout to buy me a forty, another homey passed me a blunt. I didn't hesitate to drink and smoke my reality away.

The bud had me drifting back to my cousin Champ. Man, he'd have rolled with me today, no doubt. Champ wasn't just an athlete, he was the protector. I still see us at Crystal's skating rink, stomping out that clown who teased Leslie. Champ was supposed to be in the NBA right now. Life be robbing the wrong ones.

While the fellas chopped it up about some honeys they had met the night before at the 9:30 Club, I leaned on the payphone, high sinking in, mind floating when a silver Benz crept up, rims spinning like a music video. I winced my eyes.

"Yo, is that five-o?" I nudged Marlo, who just finished shooting a game of craps.

He squinted, still shaking dice in his hands. "Nah, that's Scorpio. He got that new whip last week. But good lookin' out, Lucci." He tapped my fist, walked back toward the other fellas.

Scorpio hopped out the passenger seat like he was stepping onto a red carpet. I almost choked on my forty when I saw who got out the driver's side—Rob, Ling's little dollar-store bodyguard. Guess he was promoted to Scorpio's chauffeur. His whole vibe was sidekick energy. The man should drop "Robert" and go with "Robin." Like Batman and Robin.

Dudes swarmed Scorpio the second he pulled up, cheesin' like Snoop Dogg just stepped out the TV. Gassing his head up about his kicks, his new ride, even the shine on his watch. I just stared like *look at this hot bama flexin' like he invented oxygen.* The whole time he frontin' his new money like it came with a crown.

I never liked Scorpio. I only seen him a few times back in the day, but even then, I knew he couldn't be trusted. Always tryna act like Turk's muscle, like he was auditioning for Kingpin of the Year. He was always over the top for no reason. I swear he'd been waiting for Turk to go to prison just so he could take the throne. Seeing him now? He was the same hot clown at a different circus.

I finished the rest of the forty and dropped it on the curb. I could feel my body jerking a little with paranoia creeping in from the beer and bud doing a tag-team in my system. And with the way Rob beefed with me earlier, I figured he might want revenge. I eased across the street toward my car. *Better grab my heat.*

My hand just hit the door handle when I sensed someone behind me.

"Well, if it ain't Lil' Lucci still drivin' a bucket. Man, it's '93. Time to trade that '90 Lexus in and upgrade your life."

I turned. *Scorpio*. Out of all the dudes out here, how he spot *me*?

"You see *I* upgraded," he nodded toward his whip.

Of course he saw me. He was a clout-chasing vulture who sniffed attention like a bloodhound and noticed I was the only one who didn't clap.

He kept talking about things that didn't matter to me, just running his mouth. Every time he shifted or moved, the streetlights caught his jewelry and made it shine, almost like he was trying to show off on purpose.

"By the way, I heard you and a couple of homies got axed today," he mentioned, toothpick hanging off his lip like he chewed swagger for breakfast.

"So!" I tried to keep my voice firm, even though my head wobbled from the buzz. I wanted him to know I didn't care that he knew. I feared child support more than him.

"Whatchu mean, *so*?" He brushed a piece of lint off his Polo shirt like I was the lint. "I was gonna offer you a corner. But after the disrespect? Nah… offer revoked."

I jerked my head back. "What, you expect me to kiss the ring? Nigga, I ain't your fan."

"Oh, so it's like that?" He stepped closer, standing a few inches taller than me, but so what? I ain't care.

"I'm trying to help you, and you bite my hand?"

"I'm not your problem. And I ain't no charity case." I mean-mugged him.

On any other day, I probably would've backed down given his rep, but with everything already in shambles, I felt like I had nothing left to lose.

"You think you tough now?" he sneered. "You still the same dusty lil' bum who used to wash cars while his mother shot dope. Can't even pick up trash without gettin' fired. You was a bum lil' nigga then, and you still one now."

The words landed hard, dragging me straight back to childhood. Back to being talked to like I was nothing. Like I chose a strung-out mother. Like I never stood a chance. Everybody told me I wasn't gonna be nothing. Before I could stop myself, my hands curled into fists.

"Aww, you gon' hit me punk?" Scorpio leaned in, his breath hot, his eyes ice-cold. "Let me do you one better."

He moved fast. I was high and couldn't see it coming. Two swift uppercuts lit my ribs on fire, then a punch across my jaw sent sparkles across my eyes. I saw my whole timeline scramble—the past, present, and future. My knees gave out, and I hit the street beside my own tire. World spinning like a scratched CD. My high ran off like it had warrants. I heard the fellas sigh, *"Daaaayum!"*

From the ground, I watched Scorpio stroll back to the corner boys like he just swatted a fly. Dudes around him stiffened like they were scared they were next.

"Always correct disrespect the first time so it don't happen again," he told his runners, spitting on the ground like the whole city was his trash can.

Rob chimed in loud on purpose to make sure I could hear him. "He was overdue for that KO. You showed him why you used to be a golden-glove boxer. That sucker tried to act hard at Ling's shop. I would've popped him if his lil' shorty wasn't in my arms." He shot me a look like, *yeah, you better stay down.*

I forced myself to memorize every word, every face, every smirk. It was going to be fuel for a hardcore track later, but for now, I closed my eyes. Too weak to get up. *God, do you hate me or what?*

Just as I was thinking the wrong thoughts, I felt someone picking me up.

"I got you, bro."

I opened my eyes, feeling half-dazed. "Marlo?"

"Yeah, I got you. Scorpio didn't have to hit you like a grown man."

He grabbed my keys, put me in my seat.

"I'll drive you home. Tomorrow will be better for you, man. Just hang in there. My mom always says, God don't like ugly."

"Maybe not, but he sure ain't showed me what pretty looks like yet."

EIGHT

The Moment After

LESLIE

The second I stepped off the Greyhound bus, the humidity hit me like a wave. I smelled the salt from the bay, fried shrimp from a food truck nearby, and the faintest whiff of sunscreen from early beachgoers who were probably heading out to surf.

Mitch stood by his Jeep, sporting a Navy-style close-cut fade as he leaned casually on the hood. His blue tank top and tropical shorts showed off his maintained physique.

"There she is!" he grinned. "Miss Ivy League herself."

I blushed, thinking of the first kiss we shared at Grandma's house and how I hadn't stopped loving him since. When our eyes met, we smiled like teenagers falling in love all over again. I laughed, dragging my bags behind me.

"You make it sound like I won a beauty pageant or something."

"Nah, but you have won my heart." He pulled me in. He smelled like cocoa butter mixed with detergent. Before I could say another word, his mouth met mine. He kissed me a little too deep for public consumption, so I pulled back.

"Mmm... let's save the rest for later," I hinted.

His breath whispered against my cheek. "Can't wait."

We tossed my bags in the back of the Jeep and drove off. Top down, summer breeze in our faces, and SWV's "Right Here" thumping through the speakers. It was mid-June and later than I'd planned, but New York had me finishing up final projects with my internship program.

Mitch's condo in Virginia Beach was twenty minutes from Norfolk Naval Base, located on a narrow street near the beach. He lived upstairs, with a wraparound balcony that caught both the shoreline and the sunset views. Downstairs lived his neighbors, who he proudly introduced me to. Mr. and Mrs. Freeman. They were a nice elderly couple, who tended exotic plants in the small front yard. They took pride in showing them off when Mitch introduced us.

Inside, golden light from the sun spilled across the living room. The fridge was stacked with steaks, fancy cheeses, snacks, and one bottle of champagne, shimmering like a promise Mitch was saving just for us.

"Trying to impress me?" I teased softly.

"Always." He kissed my cheek, reached in, and took out the bottle. The cork's pop echoed through his sparsely furnished home.

"For you." He handed me a coffee mug filled with champagne.

I chuckled. "This is cute."

"Check the inscription on the side."

I read, "Coffee is the best way to silence a journalist."

We both laughed.

"This will be useful. Remind me to take it home."

"Will do. Follow me, my lady," Mitch said in a playful British accent.

We sat on the loveseat facing the TV in an otherwise bare living room. After a few more drinks, our laughter faded into softer, flirtatious conversation. As evening settled in, we found ourselves gazing into each other's eyes. Mitch gently cupped my face, as if he was trying to remember something he never wanted to forget, and then kissed me softly at first, then with fuller passion, like he was rediscovering my taste. It wasn't long before he wanted to continue in the bedroom, so he led me down a short hallway.

Chopper, Mitch's Great Dane, perked up at the foot of the bed, giving us a look that all but asked if he really had to leave. Mitch didn't say a word. He just snapped his fingers and pointed toward the living room. Chopper hopped down and trotted out obediently, and Mitch closed the door behind him.

As soon as it clicked shut, I slipped my arms around Mitch's neck. We picked up right where we'd left off, kissing slowly and tenderly. Our hands loosened each other's clothing piece by piece until each one drifted to the floor like a trail of fallen petals.

Mitch hovered over me. The look in his eyes alone made me feel beautiful and cherished; despite feeling self-conscious about the weight I'd gained through stress eating. His touch traced my curves like he was writing poetry, as if my size didn't matter to him. Every kiss he planted on my neck, my shoulders, breasts, and other places he wanted to explore, felt like he was saying, *I'm here. I've missed this. I've missed you. ALL of you.*

Our bodies fell into an unrushed rhythm that was gentle and steady, like a song we both knew by heart. His fingers intertwined with mine. His soft breaths brushed my ear as his heartbeat thudded softly against mine. And when I moved above him, confident in my ability, his face curved into a daring smirk. Whoever doubted a big girl couldn't be this flexible had never met me. I proved to Mitch that I could take charge. John Wayne could tip his hat and step aside.

As a fan blew from one of the windows, our breaths, our touches, the rising tempo of two hearts remembered how perfectly we fit together. The intensity built like a tide rolling in. Mitch's hands tightened on my waist, a breathless, vulnerable sound escaping his throat. My name fell from his lips in a soft gasp of surrender, inspiring something deeper inside me. Heat rushed through us like the sky cracked open, releasing a shower of stars. A galaxy unfurled between us as our bodies moved in waves, and Mitch felt so *Oh*-mazing.

Wait. Wait. WAIT. Why does this feel a little too…smooth?

I eased off him, glowing with a thin film of sweat. When I looked down, everything inside me dropped. Panic flooded my veins like ice water.

"Oh no. No. NO. Mitch, look!"

Mitch blinked through the fog of pleasure and pushed up on his elbows. His eyes instantly spotted what I was looking at, his brows shot up.

"Wait a minute… what happened?" he rasped, rubbing his eyes. He reached over and turned on the small desktop light attached to the headboard. The glow revealed even more what we both hoped wouldn't be there.

The beauty of our lovemaking snapped like glass. The thing meant to shield us simply gave way and sat in the middle of the bed like a popped balloon, mocking us.

"How—how could this happen?" My voice trembled as I wrapped my arms around myself. My mind exploded in a thousand directions of mostly consequences I wasn't ready to face.

"Babe…hey… it's okay. Come here," Mitch murmured, trying to force himself upright. Fatigue hung on him like bricks. Even as he pulled me into his chest and kissed my temple, I could feel him drifting and surrendering to exhaustion, but I couldn't fall asleep. Not right now. Not with my thoughts spinning.

God… please… don't let me be pregnant right now. I'll be smarter. I promise if I'm not pregnant, I'll get married before having sex again. Just please, don't let me be pregnant.

"You okay now?" Mitch asked, sensing I was still deep in thought, but I was praying in my head.

I shrugged. "Guess so."

Mitch's arms loosened from around me. Sleep overtook him. He had held me for as long as he could before collapsing back against the pillows, snoring softly while nature played her nighttime melody outside. Ocean waves crashed. Seagulls chirped. And people laughed faintly in the background. But inside? With me? A storm had just begun, and it was loud and impossible to escape. What if I'm pregnant?

NINE

When Smart Girls Slip

RAVEN

"Oh... wow," I whispered into my new cellphone, standing dead center in Pentagon City Mall like the world had suddenly pressed pause. Leslie was calling me from Mitch's place, talking in these breathy, hush-hush tones about her and Mitch's condom accident. So, like, I tried to keep my voice calm, but inside I was spinning like a ceiling fan on high. And then, because my mouth has no filter whatsoever, I couldn't keep the secret to myself anymore.

"Les... I'm pregnant and Dawson doesn't know."

Silence. Nothing but the faint hiss of Leslie's breathing and maybe her heartbeat trying to escape her body or something. So naturally, I kept talking. Fast. Like my typical rapid-fire self.

"...and you know I never even wanted kids anyway. I hated doll babies when we were growing up, except Barbie because she had the best diva outfits. Speaking of outfits, I think I found a few sexy pieces to wear to the Mirage club tonight."

More silence.

"Jeez, I hate this for us, Les. And maybe those stupid antibiotics weakened my birth control pills? Who knows! Hello? You still there?"

Finally, her voice came in, small, shaky, and absolutely traumatized.

"This can't be happening to us, Raven. We're too smart for this."

"Smart girls make mistakes too, you know."

"I'm scared, Raven. Aren't you?"

"Scared? Girl, pah-lease! I got this figured out now. Trust!" I said adamantly, shifting my Talbots shopping bags to the other arm.

"I'm coming home tomorrow. Mitch doesn't know yet, but I need the headspace to think about what I'm going to do if I'm pregnant too."

"Finally, woo-hoo!" I nearly shouted, earning a side-eye from a woman passing by with a giant pretzel. "Can't wait to see you, Cuz. We'll figure this out together. But for now… it's our secret."

TEN

Midnight Mirage

LUCCI

Man, I'm not gonna front, I was nervous walkin' into the Mirage. Soon as I stepped in, new fans rushed to me, giving hugs, dapping me up, congratulating me. I didn't even know how to react. Thanks to my cousins, Raven and Boogie, my demo had slipped into the hands of nearly everybody they knew. Before long, it was playing on every radio station in DC, even the sister stations in B-more and VA.

Within minutes of being inside, the club owner had a bouncer track me down. He pulled me to the back and asked if I could perform "Trapped" *tonight.* I wasn't prepared to perform and had only done cypher battles when I was at the detention center in Ohio. Outside of that? Nothing!

"Cuzzo, the time is now, sweetie," Boogie said. "If you're waiting for the perfect opportunity, it may never come again."

"Alright, I'll do it." I shook the owner's hand and followed a stage manager backstage. Boogie was hot on my heels with excitement for me.

I wiped my sweaty palms on my baggy jeans, peeped through the curtains at the crowd vibin' to Rare Essence's "Lock-It," and thought, *Wow, can I really do this?* I turned to Boogie.

"Yo, go tell the DJ to blend in some hip-hop so when I hit the stage it don't throw the crowd off, know what I'm saying?"

Boogie nodded and dipped.

"Lucci Loot, one minute until showtime," the stage manager said before hurrying off to check on the lighting and other stuff.

"Boogie, how I look?"

"You good, except some of your braids came loose. Hold still."

Instantly, I felt his knuckles against my scalp as he looped the braids back into place at rapid speed.

The DJ dropped the instrumental to "Mind Playing Tricks on Me" by Geto Boys. It was the same beat I sampled for my track, just as the stage manager asked if I was ready.

"Ready as I'll ever be," I tried to sound confident, remembering the days me and Champ used to rap to Run-DMC in the back of Aunt Diane's car.

The MC gave me a dope intro, and I walked out on stage, mic in hand. I was ready.

"Throw your hands in the air, and wave 'em like ya just don't care! If you came to rock with Lucci Loot tonight, let me hear ya say, 'Oh yeah!'"

"OH YEAAAH!"

The whole crowd screamed back, hands up, feeding off my energy. I launched into my first verse, and I swear the electricity hit different. Heads noddin', people rapping along, the DJ hyping me like I was already bigger than the club. For those few minutes, the world felt like mine.

When I dropped the mic, ending the song, I scanned the crowd, and that's when it happened. Right there in the middle of the floor, a guy who looked about my age was still shouting my lyrics. A spotlight caught him, pushing his way forward, as he held a copy of my demo CD in hand. I used credit cards to spend thousands of dollars producing demo copies, sometimes even using money meant for child support so I could record hundreds of them. Seeing the young soldier holding up the disc felt amazing!

I leaned into the audience, reached out and signed the dude's

CD. A girl standing next to me asked me to sign her shirt, and I scribbled my name. She shouted like I was Michael Jackson or Prince. That moment hit me harder than any applause. My song and the way the crowd was hyped, I knew…

Yeah. I can do this rap thing for the rest of my life.

ELEVEN

The Secrets of Cousins

LESLIE

After taking a pregnancy test, I was still struggling with my emotions as Raven entered the bathroom. Grandma thought we were simply getting ready to see Mama. I washed my hands and fought back the tears. Raven quietly comforted me with a hug, letting me release my worries as I sobbed harder over her shoulder.

"It's positive?" Raven asked softly.

"I don't know yet. I'm too scared to look, but I missed my period, and I've been sick on the stomach ever since."

Raven whispered, "You know, there's a way out of this if you *are* pregnant, right?"

I stepped back and stared at her like she had two heads. "No way!"

"Suit yourself." She walked over to the mirror, pulled her makeup kit out of her Coach handbag, and powdered her face until she looked even prettier.

"Where did you put the test?" she asked, once she finished.

"Over there on the shower caddy so I could pull the curtains in case Grandma walked in."

Raven peeped at it. "It's still in testing mode, but you need to chill, Les."

"You're telling me to chill? Did you even tell Dawson you were pregnant?"

Raven's jaw tightened a moment. "Nothing to tell. Not anymore. I just…sort of…handled it on my own." She snatched her purse off the sink. Dropped her lipstick inside.

Her words stung, and I couldn't close my mouth.

She looked up at me, lashes full and thick, but her eyes pooled with tears. "Please, Les. Don't judge me."

I hugged her, even as my chest felt like it might cave in once I saw my own results.

"I don't know what to say, Rave, but are you feeling okay?"

"I will be," her voice cracked over my shoulder. "Promise you won't tell."

I stepped back and looked her in the eyes. "I promise. Blood over water, no other relationship before us."

"Alright, let's take a look at what's going on with you." Raven grabbed the pregnancy test off the caddy. I covered my eyes. Didn't want to look.

"You and Mitch are going to have a beautiful baby."

"Noooo!" I groaned, trying to keep my emotions controlled so Grandma wouldn't be alerted.

I slowly dropped my hands from my face. Tears streamed down my cheeks. Visions of becoming a future journalist faded away.

Raven handed me the test. "But *not* today. Maybe later."

I looked at it, and the single line meant negative.

"Wow, thank you, God!" I wiped my tears. Instantly feeling like a bulldozer had been lifted off me. Every muscle began to relax.

"Guess this means you're going to run back to Norfolk after we visit your mom, huh?"

I shook my head. "No, Mitch is mad at me."

"Why?"

"I need to apologize to him for leaving abruptly."

"That's it?" she twisted her face in disbelief.

"Well, we kind of argued before I left." I turned away, wrapping the pregnancy test in toilet paper before throwing it in the trash.

"About what?" Raven pressed nosily.

"I sort of told him that we can't have sex anymore until we get married."

Raven blinked like she'd been slapped. "Girl, you did WHAT?"

"I promised God so long as I wasn't pregnant right now that I would wait."

"Seriously?" she propped a hand on her hip. "Well, tell God you didn't mean it."

I chuckled. "Raven, when you make a promise to God, you're supposed to keep it."

"Girls, let's go! No need to get all pretty just to visit a mental institution!" Grandma's voice boomed from downstairs.

"Les, that's totally insane. That's like taking back a steak from a pit bull."

"You're exaggerating. Mitch will eventually understand…I hope."

She sighed. "I think you got this one wrong, but let's go before Grandma gets mad at us for taking longer."

TWELVE

The Power of Words

IRENE

My room always smelled like old mop water and flowers. The scent clung to me, even when I tried to focus on the fresh pages of the notebook Mama had bought me. I'd been writing my thoughts more before my therapy sessions. Trying to pin them down before they wriggled away into darkness again. Writing helped me stay present, since talking felt hindered.

The sound of footsteps in the hallway, followed by the jangle of keys, made me pause my pen in the middle of writing. There was a knock on my door, then slowly it slid open. A guard peeped his head inside.

"Walker? You've got visitors."

Visitors? More than one? I wonder who they are.

I stood up from the neatly made bed, clutched the notebook tight to my chest, and followed him down the hall. I walked past doors that whispered with memories, doors that sometimes seemed to breathe, and I reminded myself that those breaths were just old pipes. Still…every time I passed Room 214, I heard Percy's sinister laugh in my head. 214 was his house number. Then came the flashback…

Come on in, my dog had puppies. Since you love dogs, you can have one, he'd said, unlocking the door. Shouldn't have gone there in the middle of the night after leaving the disco, but I did.

Ladies first. Percy grinned.

I walked inside the dark house, asked where the switch was, and he said, *I like it dark.*

It was the last thing I remember before he…attacked me.

My stomach clenched at the flashback.

"What's with you and that room?" the guard asked, noticing my hands trembling. Even if I could talk, I wasn't going to tell him.

"Forgot you're one of the mute ones," he snickered. "Wish everyone else around here could keep their mouths shut, but on purpose."

I entered the visiting room, feeling a familiar rush of nervous anticipation. I slid into my usual spot at the long, square table, setting the notepad and pen down with practiced care. Mama had bought me a whole set of stationaries in pretty pastel colors with matching pens. The fluorescent lights buzzed overhead, casting a cold glow as I traced the notepad's edge and listened to the echo of my own breathing. Even though I'd been here before, my nerves still pulsed in my fingertips as I glanced toward the door, eager yet anxious about who would walk in. Footsteps sounded in the hallway. At first, it was faint, almost like a memory, then growing clearer, a chorus of different heels tangling together, making unique sounds against the polished linoleum. I wondered what group was coming.

The door creaked open and I braced myself. Perhaps it was another team of doctors coming to evaluate me again. My breath caught, nerves prickling beneath my skin. But then, relief flooded through me. It was Leslie's face that appeared, not white coats and clipped voices. Her eager, radiant smile melted my tension in an instant. The worry drained from my chest, replaced by warmth and gratitude. Leslie crossed the room without hesitation and wrapped me in a hug that smelled like home, like summer rain and the faintest perfume. I felt myself truly relax.

"Missed you, Mama," Leslie murmured, her voice soft against my ear. She then stepped aside to allow Mama and Raven to hug me next. The room warmed with their presence, and for a moment, all the distance and time faded. I could feel the heat rising in my cheeks. A flush of happiness warmed my soul. I missed my daughter and I was so glad to see her.

Leslie took a seat beside me, and Mama and Raven sat across the table from us. Leslie looked fuller, her blouse stretched tight, but I was glad to see her. Her scent blended fruit and musk, and I wondered how things were at Columbia as I prepared to speak.

Talk Irene. You can do it.

I tried to speak, but a flicker moved behind Mama and Raven. The little girl in a red dress poked out her tongue.

No. Not now. I blinked, but she stayed. *What's taking my medicine so long to kick in today?*

After small talk, with them doing the talking. Mama asked, "Irene, would you like to show Leslie and Raven what you've been doing?" She always smiled too brightly around me now when she visited. Maybe to keep me encouraged, but I hate being put on the spot like a spectacle.

Leslie and Raven exchanged glances as if they were wondering what Mama was talking about. That's when I saw not just one girl, but they multiplied now, whispering to each other, their giggles echoing faintly. In therapy, I learned when they multiplied, it was a representation of all of my emotions and anxiety. And then came another flashback. It was Diane and me as teenagers. She had convinced me to climb out of our bedroom window one summer, so we could sneak off to a party.

Come on, Irene. Don't be scared. Diane tossed her long hair over her shoulder, her mischievous grin daring me to go along with her latest scheme. She always had a way of talking me into things we weren't supposed to do, and somehow, I was the one who ended up getting punished. Mama would look at me with that disappointed sigh, reminding me that as the oldest daughter, I should have known better. Every time, after the scolding, Diane would just laugh in her infamous, carefree laugh that made it all seem like a game. She had a talent for pulling Donovan and me into her trouble, then teasing us when we took the fall. But Henry never got pulled in, and after a while, she just knew not to mess with him or even try. He warned

Donovan and me to stop letting her lead us astray, but it was always hard to resist Diane's beautiful but reckless charm.

"What did you want to show us, Mama?" Leslie turned to me and asked.

I needed something real to snap me out of my hallucination of Diane, so I opened the notebook. My hand trembled like it always did when I crossed the threshold between silence and expression. I wrote:

I miss you, Leslie. I love you and I want to come home.

Leslie gasped. Raven covered her mouth in shock. And Mama smiled with pride.

I dropped the pen. Watched *them.* The hallucination of the little girls appeared in the wings. They were watching me too. Maybe they knew this moment wasn't theirs. I blinked again, and this time they faded.

Leslie's eyes traced the words gently, as if uncovering a long-lost secret. Tearful, she whispered, "Mama, I love you too. I can't believe you wrote this." In an instant, distance between us faded, replaced by understanding and warmth.

I felt something tug in my chest, something I'd buried so deep I'd forgotten it had a name.

Longing? one of the little girls asked the other one.

Yes, that's it.

Leslie steadied her breathing. Wiped her face. "Mama... can you write more? Not now—just... someday?"

I smiled and wrote.

I want to write you at college.

"Oh Mama!" Leslie hugged me, squeezed as if I had just given her a gift she'd always wanted. "You can write me as much as you want, and I promise to write you back. You don't know how much I've wanted you to communicate something to me, even if it was just to write like this."

Something cracked open inside me, small and trembling. I wrote again, slower this time, each stroke like a prayer.

You mean everything to me, Leslie. Always have.

When Leslie read it, she broke. Not loudly. Not dramatically. Silently, like someone who'd held herself together for years and finally felt arms waiting for her. Mama reached for a handkerchief in her purse and handed it to Leslie, as happy tears streamed down her cheeks. Raven looked on, happy for us all in this moment.

Ms. Lanham, my therapist, entered the room holding a folder. It wasn't our session day. In fact, it was a Saturday, and she usually worked during the week, so I wasn't sure why she was here.

"Hello everyone," she said softly. "I hope it's okay if I join you guys for a moment."

We looked up. My eyes followed her every move.

"I'm Celestine Lanham, Irene's therapist. You're Irene's daughter, Leslie, right? I recall seeing your photos in her room," she shook Leslie's hand. "And you?"

"I'm Raven, her niece."

"Nice to meet you both in person." Ms. Lanham smiled as she eased down in a chair next to Mama. "I'd like to give you all an update right now before I go on a much-needed vacation."

I smiled, figuring out that was why she was working the weekend.

"Irene has been doing wonderfully. She's learning to wash her own clothes, sew, make snacks, and she listens and expresses herself more through writing."

"Yes, and we are so *very* proud of her." Mama beamed.

Ms. Lanham cleared her throat. "Well, although Irene has been doing well, I believe she's been saving her voice."

"For whom?" Mama asked, leaning in.

"Her sister, Diane. She mentions her often in her writings during our therapy sessions."

The room went still for a few seconds. Only the humming noise from the fan in the corner could be heard.

"Diane?" Mama whispered, and Leslie froze, clutching my notebook like it was her winning prize.

"Yes," Ms. Lanham continued. "Irene's silence hasn't been a refusal to speak nor a fear of connection. Not totally, but she hasn't seen her sister since the incident happened, correct? Privately. As in, one-on-one where the two of them could possibly talk about what happened. Am I correct?"

"I think so," Raven nodded. "My mother is scared to see Aunt Irene."

Ms. Lanham glanced at the family. "Listen, I know it's difficult, and we don't believe in meddling in family affairs, but if Diane were willing to visit Irene, we would like to observe the impact this would have on her progress. I mean, it could provide the closure she needs for her healing process."

"Or make her angry and revert back." Mama shook her head, feeling concerned.

"I don't want to push," Ms. Lanham said. "But Irene wrote *yes* when I asked her if she would be willing to meet with Diane."

"I'll talk to her, Grams. I can try to get her to come here," Raven chimed in.

"It would be long overdue. I think it's time," Leslie added.

"Your mother deserves an opportunity for closure," Ms. Lanham stated, closing the file. "Life won't be perfect for Irene, but as long as she stays on her medication and keeps up with her outpatient appointments, her doctor and I both agree she may do just fine at home."

"We want what's best for Irene," Mama stated, as if those were her final words.

"So do we, Ms. Walker." Ms. Lanham shook everyone's hand before leaving. "I hope by the time I'm back from vacation that Diane will be ready to meet. You guys seem like a really supportive and loving family, and Irene deserves to return home to you." With that, Ms. Lanham left the room.

"Well, Aunt Irene, we do need to get going," Raven said, looking just like her mother, but thank God she didn't have her selfish and devious personality. None that I could tell. She used to bring me cookies and do my makeup on special occasions.

Leslie handed me my notepad, and I wrote.

I hope to see you girls again, soon.

They smiled.

"You will," Leslie hugged me goodbye.

"See ya, Auntie. I'll tell my mom to come visit." Raven kissed my cheek.

"Stay blessed." Mama hugged me. "I'm proud of you."

When they left, I was already missing them.

Lord, please free me from this place soon. I want to be with my family.

THIRTEEN

This Side of Forever

RAVEN

"I just wonder what my mother's life is going to look like once she starts talking again," Leslie said. We were continuing our conversation after leaving St. Elizabeth Hospital and dropping off Grams at bingo.

"Same," I replied, merging onto the highway toward Dawson's place in the suburbs. "She's making good progress, but if I'm being honest, it's going to be scary for not just her, but us too. Like, we've never heard her speak or express how she feels about stuff, you know?"

Leslie nodded slowly. "I agree. I'm happy she's improving, but nervous too. I'm wondering if talking with your mom will make her spiral like Grams said? Or will it really help, like Ms. Lanham suggested."

"Not sure, but one thing I do know is that it's high time for our mothers to talk, period!"

"Tell me about it," Leslie exhaled.

For a moment, everything grew quiet with just the sound of the highway and cars driving by until Leslie spoke again.

"I really miss Mitch. He hasn't returned my calls."

"I'm sure you do."

"We left things so messy."

I glanced at her, gave her a look as if to say, *ya think?*

"Probably overreacted, but"—she lifted her hand—"that doesn't change my stance. I've had time to think and reconnect with God. I'm keeping my promise to Him."

"Uh-huh." I switched lanes, giving her a quick side-eye. "Freakin' stubborn."

"Am not. I just want things done right from now on."

"Sometimes being right, you could end up left," I said, flicking the turn signal.

Leslie huffed. "What else can I do if he won't talk to me?"

"Somebody's gotta just say it. Leave him a detailed message or write a letter or something. You're really good with words."

We exited the highway and came up to a red light. Leslie stared ahead like the whole world was in that one traffic signal.

"I don't want to lose him, Rave."

"You won't." I tapped my nails on the steering wheel, feeling a bit anxious about my own relationship.

"Hope you're right."

WHEN WE ARRIVED at Dawson's house, Snow's "Informer" played as kids ran around, adults chatted over dominoes, and the air smelled like charcoal and burgers. I waved to Dawson's parents, dodged a football, and caught Boogie low-key touching pinkies with a guy by the pool. This was Dawson's going-away party, and I wasn't ready for him to leave me.

Leslie and I found a spot at a table with Tierra and Camille, who were sitting with their new boyfriends, who happened to be Dawson's teammates from the Howard Bisons. The barbecue was just starting to settle into its groove, with laughter bouncing off the backyard walls and the smoky aroma from the grill thick in the air.

I listened as Tierra teased Camille about terrible dance moves from some party they'd gone to without me the night before. Since they were paired up now, I didn't want to be a fifth wheel. Leslie's gaze occasionally drifted toward the swimming pool, each time someone took a dive. For a moment, I just relaxed, letting the warm evening and the familiar rhythm of conversation wash over me. Then Dawson stepped out of the house, carrying a tray stacked high with desserts.

"There you are," Dawson called out, setting the tray down with a broad smile. He moved around the table, giving high fives to his teammates and fist bumps to Tierra, Camille, and Leslie before finally coming over to me. He hugged me, catching me mid-bite.

"Stop, I'm trying to finish your mom's apple salad. It's so refreshing!" I protested, nudging him with my elbow as the others laughed.

"Ask her for the recipe," Dawson said, leaning in to kiss my cheek. He pulled out a chair and sat next to me and immediately joined in on the various random conversations.

He asked Leslie about Columbia, and Tierra and Camille about their new jobs before talking basketball with his boys. He then turned toward me and squeezed my hand.

"Can I steal you for a minute?" he asked. Before I could respond he whisked me away, taking hold of my hand firmly. My fork fell to my plate. *Guess I won't finish the salad.*

We darted through clusters of people, pausing to greet an aunt or dodge a runaway toddler. The music faded as we moved toward a secluded garden nook beneath a wall of climbing vines. Dawson stopped in front of the bubbling fountain at the center of the garden and turned to me with a deep breath, letting the moment settle.

"Raven, you've been my *one* since the day I met you cheering our Bisons to victory at courtside. I love you so much."

"I… love you too," I gasped. *Where is he going with this?*

Then he knelt. Pulled out a velvet box from his pocket.

"Marry me," he said, voice steady, revealing a huge princess-cut diamond and gold ring.

My heart crashed into my ribs with too many emotions all at once. I felt love, fear, and the secret I'd kept from him. Thought about the girls I had to keep chasing away. *He's serious? Marriage? Really?*

As Dawson waited, ring shining under the garden lights, doubt tangled through my thoughts. Was I really ready for this? The memory of his cheating, hidden behind smiles and apologies, stung in the back of my mind. It felt wrong to start something as big as marriage with secrets between us. I'd spent too long pretending everything was okay, pretending I was okay, burying what I'd done and what he'd done. His betrayal and my own carried the same weight, and I couldn't let history repeat itself. I imagined saying yes and being the perfect couple that the optics would betray us to be (like my parents once were), and I was sure they'd be happy. But the words caught, stuck on the truth I'd never spoken. Was love enough if honesty didn't come first? Marriage should be a clean slate, not another chapter of lies. I needed to be real, even if it risked losing him. In that moment, I realized I couldn't keep my secret any longer. He deserved to know, and I deserved to be free from the guilt I'd been carrying.

"But what about Italy?" I blurted.

"It's just for the summer. I'll be back just in time to start our wedding plans. Gonna be so fly to have a woman like you as my bride."

A woman like me? What does that mean? He didn't even sound sincere, and I couldn't keep pretending. Not with that beautiful ring staring at me.

"Dawson," I said, voice tiny. "There's something you should know."

As I began to explain what I had done, his expression slowly began to crack like ice breaking. He stood up slowly and looked stunned. His eyes widened in disbelief, long thick brows lifting in shock, and his mouth hung slightly open, as if he was searching for words that wouldn't come. For a moment, all expression drained from his face except for the raw surprise, leaving him frozen and speechless.

"Why—why would you do something like that?" he asked, teary-eyed.

"I was scared, Dawson. I didn't want you to think I was trying to trap you or ruin your basketball dreams." My voice wobbled.

He snapped the velvet box closed, hard. Like a door slamming to a final, freakin' ending.

"What you did was selfish… and—and… cruel!" Dawson's voice trembled.

"What did that make you when you kept cheating on me?" I shot back because my mouth moves to every emotion I feel, even when it hurts.

"You can't compare what I did to what you did. That's not fair."

"Fair? How many women have you been with since we've been together, huh?"

"Raven, are you sick? Because you can't compare that to destroying a life."

His words broke me, making it hard for me to breathe. Tears rose in my eyes, and when I blinked, they spilled. He was right. I'd crossed the line.

"I'm sorry. I just…thought I was doing the right thing for both of us. We weren't ready to have kids. You know that Dawson."

I stepped back. Stared at the fountain as water arched into the evening air, shimmering as the soft lights glowed from beneath. Ripples danced across the surface, and every so often, the jets shot a little higher, sparkling in the glow. The fountain's peaceful rhythm stood in stark contrast to the turmoil written all over Dawson's face.

"So, how do we fix this?" I asked softly, breaking the moment of silence.

He glared, his body tense, and his voice shook slightly. "Fix? You already did."

With that, Dawson stormed off, tossing the velvet box over the fence because he could be just as dramatic and spoiled as me.

I stood there feeling numb, not knowing what to do next.

When I returned to the cookout, people were already packing up. I watched as foil folded over plates, chairs stacked, the night quietly winding down. Maybe the tension showed on my face, because Dawson's mom noticed it right away.

"Everything okay?" she asked softly.

I murmured a quiet yes and headed for my car to wait for Leslie. From the corner of my eye, I saw Dawson standing with his father near the grill. Both tall, broad-shouldered, sharing the same imposing height, though their complexions differed.

Dawson and his dad spoke in low tones, shaking their heads like men trying to make sense of something that had gone wrong. I couldn't tell what Dawson had told him. Maybe about the proposal. About how it was supposed to go… and how it didn't. I could tell that phone calls were probably going to be made tonight. Mom calling my cell telling me, "You blew it, Raven, Dawson comes from money," or Dad saying, "Did you have to be brutally honest?" I knew from prior breakups those would be their reactions. I didn't want a trophy anymore, I wanted love.

As I sat behind the wheel, memories of Dawson flooded me. Our relationship was always a seesaw of good days and bad, passion and friction. I used to believe our disagreements made us real, and that love wasn't meant to be perfect. I also convinced myself that Dawson's cheating was because I didn't give him enough sex, but even when I did, he kept cheating anyway. The bigger question is, *why do I always stay?* Taj did the same thing to me in high school, but I still stayed.

When Leslie pulled the door handle and climbed inside, I told her that Dawson and I had broken up. She listened and expressed sympathy in a way that she always did. Like a big sister, she ended with, "Let's grab an ice cream cone from *Friendly's.*" I glanced at her, and although I forced a smile through my pain, inside I was torn.

Ending things with Dawson brought relief somewhat. But what I did was stuck to me like thick Velcro. I hoped that one day Dawson would forgive me like the numerous times I'd forgiven him, and that we could one day be friends again. If not for what I did, then for who I was when I did it.

FOURTEEN

We Can't Be Friends

MITCH

Chopper whined at the door again with his tail wagging rapidly, but I didn't move. The couch felt too comfortable. A haze of cigarette smoke clouded the living room. I'd quit the habit before, but the minute Leslie and I fell apart, I did too. Empty beer bottles rolled when I shifted my foot, reminding me I had drunk too many. This wasn't how I pictured my summer. Not by a long shot.

The phone rang. *Leslie* lit up the caller ID for what felt like the fiftieth time. What was there to say? She'd gone home to DC after telling me she thought she was pregnant, then swore off sex. There wasn't even a discussion about it. No warning. No *what do you think, Mitch?* Just—boom. A grenade tossed into the middle of everything we'd been building and the beautiful summer I had planned for us.

The phone rang again, insistent. Chopper barked once, like he was telling me to stop being stupid and respond to the phone call or to *him*. I shut my eyes, exhaling smoke and frustration at the same time.

"Alright," I muttered, not even sure who I was talking to, myself or Chopper. I leaned over reluctantly and grabbed the phone.

"What do you want, Leslie?"

A shaky exhale came through the line. "Mitch…please…please don't hang up."

I didn't answer. My jaw was locked too tight to trust my own voice.

"I know you're upset," she said softly. "I handled things badly."

My hand dragged down my face. "You dropped a bomb and walked off. What was I supposed to do with that?"

"But I'm calling to explain," her voice was small and pleading.

I leaned back deeper into the couch, into the ache sitting in my chest. "Alright. Explain."

She hesitated just long enough for me to picture her pacing the room the way she does when she's nervous.

"I know I shouldn't have made that promise to God without talking to you first. I apologize for that."

"Wild guess says you aren't pregnant after all, right?"

"No…I'm not." She paused just enough for me to hear the theme song to *Living Single* playing from her TV in the background. "But I am sticking to my promise."

I sat forward, elbows on my knees. "Then why are you calling me? Because right now, I'm confused."

"I feel like I owe you an explanation, but not an ultimatum. Maybe it came across that way."

"Not worse than you making me feel like us making love was wrong. We're two consenting adults."

"But Mitch, I—"

"No, listen, Les, you need to hear this because your explanation makes zero sense." I forced myself to stand. "I've loved you since we were kids. When I was in San Diego and you were in New York, we made it work. Soon as I could, I moved back East. I moved back to *you.* You know why? Because I believed in what we were building. I thought you believed in us too."

"I did," she insisted. "I mean, I still do."

"No, you don't, Les. If you believed in us, you would've stayed. Don't you trust me enough to know that if you were pregnant, I wouldn't have bailed on you?"

"Of course I do."

"Then why would you treat me like I was some random guy you slipped up with? This is me—Mitchell Larson. The same guy who saved you and your family when your house caught on fire."

"I didn't want you to try to change my mind and make me break my promise, so I left."

Ouch. She thought I'd make her fight her faith instead of walking with her through it? I exhaled hard, nothing left to argue. I snatched another cigarette from the pack. *Crap! My last one.*

"I'm not going to force you to propose, Mitch."

"But you *are* asking me to accept a decision that didn't involve me. You axed me out of the picture. Forgot the type of man I am."

Little sniffles came through the phone, and something inside me folded. I shouldn't have raised my voice at her, but I'm hurting. I wanted so badly to stay mad, to protect myself. But hearing her cry? It softened every hard edge I'd tried to keep.

Chopper trotted over and nudged my knee, picking up on the storm inside me. I clipped the leash on him so I could prepare to take him out.

"I'm sorry, Mitch. I didn't mean to bail on you in that way. I panicked, that's all," Leslie said softly. I knew she meant it, but what happened still hurt.

I snuffed out the cigarette in the ashtray, exhaling smoke through my nose. "Yeah, you did, but you're still keeping that promise." I smirked behind the phone.

"I have to," she sounded determined or better yet, stubborn.

"Yeah, well, that's your promise, not mine."

"What is that supposed to mean?" she asked as I stood and walked to my front door, cordless phone cuffed under my ear.

"It means..." I unlocked the door. "I don't know how to be in this relationship anymore. I can't just pretend like we weren't already intimate. I'm a man with needs."

"The Navy taught you how to be disciplined. Aren't you willing to try?" she asked, voice breaking apart again.

I shut my eyes for a brief moment before opening the door. I tried to imagine holding back to honor her promise and deny my desires, but doubt was already cracking the picture.

"I don't think I'm capable of what you're asking me."

"If that's what you want, then—"

"Oh no, no, no." I wasn't about to let her lay a guilt trip on me. "None of this is what *I* wanted for us." My voice stood firm. "None of it."

"Fine!" Her voice rose an octave, matching mine. "I guess this is goodbye then."

My throat closed up. I didn't want to say it, but the writing was on the wall. I opened the door, stepped out. "Guess it is."

We both hung up. I tossed the phone over my shoulder. Not caring where it landed.

Chopper nudged his head into my leg, picking up on the pain I was feeling. We stepped outside together, and as soon as we made it down the steps and out the main door, Chopper took care of his business. Suddenly, he spotted a squirrel and, in a flash, bolted after it. My heart was too heavy to react. I just stood there, rooted to the spot, watching as the squirrel darted into the street. A car screeched around Chopper, narrowly missing him, while the squirrel reached the opposite curb, scrambled up a tree, and disappeared onto a high branch, safe and far out of reach.

"CHOPPER, GET OVER HERE—NOW!" Panic snapped me out of my fog.

He ran back toward me, leash dragging behind him like no never mind. I grabbed it and tugged him back inside. "You know better than that. I can't lose you too."

My phone was ringing again when I walked through the door. I hurried over, a small part of me hoping it was Leslie calling back. The caller ID read: *Jennifer Gregg.* I frowned. Scratched my temple. *Who is that?*

"Hello?" I answered, tightening my brow suspiciously.

"Hi there, can I speak to Mitch, please?"

"Speaking."

"Hey, it's Jenny. We met at Pete's party a few weeks ago."

I thought about it. *The pretty redhead with green eyes.*

"Oh, hey, what's up?"

"We're going to Quigley's tonight to watch the baseball game and have a few beers. Care to join us?"

"Uhm...sure, yeah, why not?"

"Awesome. See you at seven."

I hung up. I really wanted to stay home and shut out the world. Just like at my shipmate Pete's party when I first met Jenny. She tried to cheer me up that night. She was Pete's girlfriend's bestie or whatever. We danced a couple of times. Exchanged numbers. But I never thought much of it after that.

Sitting alone again tonight would only give me too much room to feel the gloom. I caught a glimpse of the old scars on my wrists. Couldn't let myself spiral like that again. I'd been down that road before. When Angel and I broke up years ago, the pain had dragged me so deep I'd honestly thought I might never climb back out.

The Navy had drilled one thing into me besides discipline: when life throws a curveball, you don't stand still and get hit. You dodge, adjust, and keep moving. So, I showered, got dressed, and headed out. I decided to force myself to enjoy what was left of summer, even if the person who mattered most was missing.

FIFTEEN

Boys and Beats

LUCCI

Props to Aunt Diane for hooking me up with her lawyer friend. Summer came and went, but she helped me fight to get Lucci on weekends cuz Ling still on drama. She makin' my life miserable. Should have formed an alliance with Trojan!

Despite finding another job, she tried to get more money for child support, knowing my new job delivering bottled water was only part time. I'm tryna' find another gig to make ends meet, but she don't understand that. Thanks to Ling's being greedy, I had to use half the money I made off "Trapped" to pay the lawyer. Can't catch a break, man. Now I'm up here writing more rhymes, hoping to earn another local hit while my boys are playing.

The basement was scattered with toys as the two brothers were happy to be back together. Maybe *too* happy.

"Ay yo! Y'all slow down!" I yelled, making sure they wouldn't knock over my CD towers and music equipment while they ran around with a football. Both of them just turned three, and with their little innocent eyes, they paused for a moment, looked at me, and went right back to chasin' each other and screaming. Hardheaded!

"Be glad when y'all mothers come and get y'all," I mumbled

under my breath, from the pullout sofa. Between the music and my boys playing, if I didn't happen to look up, I wouldn't have seen my cordless phone lighting up. The caller ID read: *Unknown Caller.*

I hesitated at first, thinking it may be a bill collector, and I should just let G-Ma answer the phone from upstairs, but then I thought, *I'll grab that joint.*

"Hello?" I answered with caution.

"Hi, is this Lucci?"

"Depends on who's asking."

"This is Amanda Walsh. I'm the secretary at Midtown Records."

I sat straight up so fast my pen rolled off the sofa. "Did you say Midtown?"

I waved to my boys, hissing and telling them to knock it off so I could hear.

"Yes, and I'm calling on behalf of Sheldon Steiner, our A and R Director. His daughter saw you performing at the Mirage in DC last summer. She recorded it and showed him the video. He loved your performance."

"Thanks." I smiled to myself. *That was in the summer and it's December now. What took him so long if he liked my performance?*

"Is 'Trapped' yours? Did you write it?" Amanda continued.

My heart did a whole spin with pride. "Yeah," I said. "That's all me. I wrote it."

I heard typing on her end. She was calm and professional, like she did this stuff all the time.

"Great. Do you have more songs? Enough for a full album?"

"Yeah, yeah, I got plenty of tracks. Some polished, some rough, but I got hella material."

"That's what Mr. Steiner would want to hear."

I was cheesing like a mug behind the phone.

"Mr. Steiner wants to invite you to our talent night next Wednesday at eight p.m. He'd love to meet the face and voice behind that performance. We were all impressed by your stage presence and the way you owned the crowd."

I stood, legs shaking. "Wait… you serious?"

"Very serious," she said. "Can you make it next week?"

I opened my mouth to answer and then, a disaster happened in real time. Little Lucci's foot clipped the phone cord as he was running from Donovan. The whole cordless base tumbled, plug popped out the wall, as Little Lucci hit the floor.

The phone died. Just gone.

"NO—WHAT THE—COME ON, MAN!"

I stared at the dark screen of the phone in my hand. Pressing buttons like I could make that joint come back to life. Furious, I yelled, "LUCCI! GET UP!"

He froze. His half-lidded eyes widened, lips trembled. His brother Donovan started crying at the sound of my voice. He knew he was in trouble, too. I snatched my belt off in pure frustration.

"No, Dad-dee!" they both cried, pointing at each other in blame.

I dropped my belt. Feeling guilty as I thought of how my mom used to beat me, and how I promised I'd never do that to my kids.

"What's all that hollerin' down there?" G-Ma shouted from upstairs.

"Go upstairs with your great-granny! MOVE!" I pointed.

They scrambled up sniffling and walked up the stairs. I overheard G-Ma say, "Don't cry, it's alright, Nana's here." Spoiling them like she always do.

I grabbed the phone base, plugged everything back in. My hands were shaking like I just got shocked. The phone lit up—*Unknown Caller* flashing again. I hit the talk button so hard I almost broke it.

"Hello? HELLO?!"

"It's Amanda again," she said, kinda laughing. "Sounds like one of your little ones got too excited."

"Yeah, somethin' like that." I rubbed the sweat beads off my forehead. "I'm sorry about that."

"No worries. If you have a pen, I can give you all the details."

I wrote everything down carefully from the address, phone number, and what time I needed to be there.

"Man," I said, exhaling hard. "This is crazy. I always see y'all's ads in *The Source* magazine, but never in my life thought Midtown would call *me*."

"You can thank Sarah. She's Mr. Steiner's daughter, when you meet her."

"Amanda, real quick, let me ask you something." I scratched my temple. "If Mr. Steiner likes my performance, what's gonna happen next?"

"Lucci, if Mr. Steiner likes you, you're not going back home unless *you* decide to. Do you understand what that means?"

"I think so."

"Between us, you've got nothing to worry about. I don't say this often, but I have a really good feeling about you. So, pack your bags. Kiss your old life goodbye."

"Thank you, Amanda. For real. I'll see y'all next Wednesday."

As soon as I hung up, I looked up at the ceiling like God Himself was about to poke His head through. Then before I could get all excited and do a happy church dance, something clicked. *How am I gonna get to New York?*

I called Aunt Diane and explained everything.

"Am I your ATM machine, Lucci?" she shouted after I asked for help. Gave me her usual *I can't keep helping you* lecture before she caved anyway.

"I'll wire you the money tomorrow, but if this music thing doesn't pan out, you owe me. I expect you to clean my house top to bottom and wash my cars for a month."

"Dang, Auntie. Maybe I should just hitchhike to New York."

"Boy, get off my phone. Bye."

CLICK.

I laughed after she hung up like she ain't care. She loved me, always have. Even when my mother's old boyfriend Earl and I got into it, Aunt Diane was right there. Saved my life even when I got in trouble and dudes thought I killed my homies Mook and Peanut. But now? I finally had something to make all of them proud of me. This was my chance to see if I could finally do something right with my life, and I was ready!

PART II

And Then This Happened...

SIXTEEN

The Scorpion and the Frog

RAVEN

"Leslie is going all out with her religious endeavors," I said to Boogie as I turned the steering wheel to switch lanes. "She came home last weekend just to get baptized. And can you believe she broke up with Mitch over her promise? Seriously, there is no way I'm letting a man that fine get away over a few shouts and a tambourine."

"Why are you talking like I wasn't there? And don't be mad at Leslie because you're a heathen," Boogie said, rolling his neck.

"I am not!"

"Indeed, you are, honey, and so am I. You dress yours up with red-bottom heels and Prada bags while I own mine." He flipped through the CDs in my brand-new Beamer. It was a gift from my father for crushing it this sophomore year thus far. Funny how not having a boyfriend has made me more focused.

"Can't believe Grams called us out here today anyway," I grumbled.

"Me neither," Boogie echoed, turning up the heat. Winters were always hard on Boogie's asthma, but he insisted on coming with me to pick up Grams to take her grocery shopping at Giant Food, her favorite spot to shop.

Last night, we went to the Classic Nightclub for my 20th birthday. I got in by flirting with the bouncer; Boogie knew the other bouncer from Tracks. We didn't drink, but still had fun, and stayed over at my parents' house in Brandywine. Grams called early wanting a ride to shop since her car was acting up again.

"You talked to Nicki?"

"No."

"Do you know how the baby's doing?"

"Nope."

"Boogie! Are you insane? You need to go check on your baby after this."

"Girl, hush up and apply for that new program."

"Program? What are you talking about?"

"You haven't heard? It's free, and it's called Mind Your Business."

I rolled my eyes. "Whatever!"

"Ever since you and Dawson broke up, you've been nonstop in other people's business."

"You sound like an old lady."

"No, but I'm an educated queen, boo."

I shook my head and laughed.

Boogie and I sang along to Toni Braxton, cruising the highway until a yellow glow caught my eye, it was the gas light. I clucked my teeth. We just hit DC, but I always panicked when the gas light came on. I wondered if we'd make it over the Sousa Bridge to Grams. Couldn't be sure since I was still learning the car.

Reluctantly, I pulled into the sketchy gas station on Minnesota Avenue across the street from Mario's Pizza. It's the same station that no one ever liked to get gas from unless they wore a bulletproof vest. You know, the kind of spot where the air smells like motor oil and trouble. And pumping gas in the middle of February wasn't exactly my idea of having a fun Saturday. With Boogie's asthma, the dirty work fell on me.

I slipped out into the wind, heeled boots crunching against icy pavement, as the air slapped me in the face, not even caring about my new MAC makeup. Shivering, I shoved the nozzle into the tank and tightened my short mink coat at the neck.

The pump started, and I dashed back into the car to thaw while it filled automatically. Toni was on her next track, "Seven Whole Days," and Boogie was singing every word, shoulders rocking a mellow pace to the rhythm.

THONK. THONK. THONK.

"What was that?" Boogie and I jolted, instinctively looking behind us when we heard the loud thud.

I cautiously stepped out, wishing I had pepper spray just in case. "Boogie, you stay inside. It's too cold for you," I said as he attempted to get out. Wished he'd stayed at my house. He could be stubborn like Leslie. Maybe it runs in the family.

"Bout time you got out!" A tall young man, who looked to be in his late twenties, pulled the nozzle free from my tank; gas was spilling everywhere since it didn't automatically click off like I'd hoped. The sharp fumes from the spill stung my nose and quickly filled the air.

"Oh no! I'll go get some help!" I hurried to the station booth and told the station attendant they needed cleanup at pump five, then paid for my gas.

The cold wind practically blew me back to the car.

"You can't say thank you?" The man's tone was cocky. "I just saved you from turning this station into a fireball."

"Excuse me?"

"I saved you while you were busy listening to Toni Braxton," he said with enough force to command my attention. His stare was magnetic. Like he was trying to read my thoughts. He didn't look unkind or uncaring, but careful, like he was assessing.

Before I could respond, a station attendant hustled over with a wad of rags, muttering something about "kids who don't watch what they're doing." He bent low and scrubbed the Beamer's side panel until it shined like new. I dug five dollars from my coat pocket and pressed it into his hand for his efforts.

The mysterious guy watched my every move, leaning against the driver's side of his spotless black 4Runner at the pump behind mine.

His dark complexion caught the sunlight, revealing some of his softer and more handsome features. Kind of reminding me of Wesley Snipes, by his eyes. Something about the way he stared.

"You can tip him easily, but a brother like me had to remind you to have manners?"

My eyes widened. "Dude, what is your problem?" I asked, slinging my hair over my shoulder to keep the wind from blowing it into my eyes again.

"I don't like ungrateful people."

I shoved my hands into my coat pockets, fished around for more money, but didn't feel anything to give to him, so I said, "For what it's worth, thank you for your help."

That earned a slight grin that wasn't warm or cold but controlled.

"Was that hard to say?"

"No, but it wasn't easy either," I shot back, grabbing the handle of my car door to step inside.

"Ay yo, hold up. What's your name?" he called out, removing the nozzle from his truck, returned it quickly to the pump.

"Raven."

"Hmmm. Raven? Like a bird," he repeated, like he was savoring it.

"And yours?" I asked, crossing my arms, feeling curious as to how this would play out, despite being cold.

"Scorpio," he stated, adjusting the gold chain adorned with a scorpion pendant. His Coogi sweater complemented his blue jeans and goose down coat. However, it was his name that made me recall where I'd heard it. Accounts from the community and stories from folks in Grams's neighborhood depicted him as a guy you didn't want to mess with. I also recalled Boogie's personal account that Scorpio had once saved his life with a few words.

"Is it true what folks say about you, *Scorpio*?"

"Depends on what they're saying."

"You mean it depends on *who's* asking."

That earned a deep, smooth laugh. The kind that sounds like it surrendered after an argument.

He opened the door to his truck, leaned in, pulled out a pen and a torn piece of paper, and walked over to me.

"Write your number down." It wasn't a question, but a demand. I kind of liked it. Wrote it down. He tucked it in his pants pocket.

"Deuces." He flipped the peace sign with his two fingers, took a few steps back to his truck.

"Wait! That's it?" I asked. "No smooth one-liner like, 'You're beautiful and I'll call you at seven?'"

"You gave me what I wanted. Nothing else to say."

I walked toward him. My pulse skipped. "And if you don't call me. How can I reach *you*?"

"You need to earn that first. I don't give out my number easily."

I stood there stunned but thrilled at the same time, with my mouth gaped open. *Earn it? Hmm…*

"I'll be in touch," he said, starting the engine. Snoop Dogg's "Gin and Juice" came through the speakers blasting. I stepped back toward my car. Watched him drive off full speed, like he was in a hurry and I was already yesterday's news.

Inside the car, the warm air engulfed me like a long-lost friend. I eased out of the station but could feel Boogie's eyes on me. I glanced at him.

"What?"

"You do realize who that was, right?"

"Now I do."

Boogie shook his head. "Scorpio is a warning sign for trouble. You don't want none of that. Trust and believe me."

"Boogie, relax. I'm a big girl who can handle myself."

"You just want some of that chocolate, don't you?"

I blushed.

"He's not your type," he said adamantly. "Men like Scorpio don't raise their voices, but they do raise other kinds of hell. Don't say I didn't warn you."

"I've been warned." I arched my brow. "Maybe it's time I live on the edge a little. I'm always with smart pretty boys. A bad boy could be fun."

"Moths that fly too close to the flame get burned."

"I won't."

SEVENTEEN

Baby Mama Drama

BOOGIE

I don't even roll through Simple City anymore, not unless I got that sketchy little pistol Lucci slid to me, right before he dipped to New York chasing some wild dream. Child, I keep that thing gripped tight in my coat like it's the only accessory that matters. Out here, hustlers got the courtyard jumping, serving up junkies like it's a brunch buffet. First of the month, March, and honestly? Every time I come to see my daughter, my chest gets all tight and anxious. Between this mess and the vibe out here, I hate that she's stuck living in this place. But honey, what am I supposed to do? I'm hustling classes, dance gigs, and trying to figure myself out. It ain't like I can afford to change her world…yet.

I hadn't seen my baby since she was basically burrito sized. She arrived in November, and between my freshman classes at Howard and Spirit of Washington dance gigs with the Rhythm Rock Boys, my schedule's more packed than a Popeye's drive-thru on a Sunday after church. Mom's like, "Boogie, she's your responsibility, not ours," and Dad's threatening to make me a fry cook if I don't step up. They're back together now. Some days, I think about living on campus just to escape my parents' tag-team lectures. My major?

Haven't decided. Not unless dance battles count. Still, the guilt dragged me here, nerves doing the cha-cha in my chest.

Nicki finally cracked open the door with all the enthusiasm of someone opening their phone bill. My palms were already sweating like I'd been dunked in a hot yoga class, and my brain was running marathons, desperately searching for an excuse to dodge the incoming roast session. Just yesterday we were besties. We moved like peanut butter and jelly, now we're peanut butter and, I don't know…kale?

She gives me the same look my dad throws when he catches me bringing home a girl one night and a dude the next, as if I'm the most confusing riddle. Like some wild SAT logic question nobody can solve.

All my nerves were tangled up in knots from the minute I stepped inside, and Nicki was rolling her eyes at me and complaining under her breath before I even sat down good. I said nothing back, just took my coat off and sat while she held our daughter in her arms.

The aroma of Ms. Jackson frying chicken hung in the air. The sweet, seasoned smell of that batter made my stomach growl. I was so hungry my stomach felt like it was pushed to my back, but I knew if I stopped somewhere to eat, I'd change my mind about coming over here. And I knew better than to get my hopes up to Ms. Jackson offering me a drumstick or a wing. Ever since Nicki got pregnant, Ms. Jackson made it clear I was just barely tolerated and definitely not family. She caught my eye from the kitchen, and honey, let me tell you, her look could've wilted a bouquet of flowers. I shrank back, wishing I could disappear into the freakin' wall.

"Nicki, remind your baby's daddy that you haven't seen him in almost four months." Ms. Jackson's voice boomed from the kitchen, like I wasn't right there in her living room.

My cheeks burned. This was why, back when things first got ugly, I suggested to Nicki that maybe adoption was a better option for us. Honey, that fight was legendary! I woke up to find my brand-new Toyota Corolla (a high school graduation gift from my parents) had been keyed. You can guess who did it. Not to mention, Ms.

Jackson called me and absolutely lost it over the phone. She yelled, "Nicki will not put her baby up for adoption!"

I just sat on the phone, jaw clenched, not daring to hang up on her out of respect, but in short, I knew not to ever suggest adoption again. If my ears didn't ring with pain for days, the agony of seeing the scratches on my car did.

Nicki glared at me, repeating her mother's words with ice-cold precision. "Where have you been, Boogie?"

I took off my new goose down coat, avoided direct eye contact with her as I replied, "I been around." Pulled a pair of booties out of the gift bag that Grandma crocheted. Hoped it'd smooth things over.

"Indy was sick and needed medicine!" Nicki exclaimed, cradling Indigo in the fold of her arms. We called her "Indy" for short. Her name was the only thing we'd agreed on. Indigo Blair Walker. She was four months, I think, since she was born in November and it was March. Not sure.

Nicki shifted closer holding Indy, who reminded me of one of those Monchhichi dolls from the '80s. She was adorable and innocently wide-eyed. She had soft curls that were thick around the crown of her head and ears pointy like mine. She was definitely bigger than the last time I'd seen her, back when she was only a few weeks old.

Tiny beads of sweat glistened on Indy's forehead. She was bundled too tight. Between the heat blasting from the vents and her grandmother cooking in the kitchen, even I was starting to feel overheated.

"Maybe you should take the blanket off her," I suggested quietly.

The moment Nicki loosened the wrap, Indy's face scrunched, and she let out a sharp cry. Instinct took over. I reached for her, cradled her against my chest, and began rocking her until the crying softened into hiccupping breaths.

That's when the clatter started from the kitchen. Pots slamming, metal ringing against metal. I looked up just as Ms. Jackson came charging in from the kitchen.

"Now listen to me, Boogie." She pointed at me before planting a firm hand on her hip. Ms. Jackson was tall, light-skinned, and big-boned. The kind of woman who looked like she could take Hulk Hogan in a fight and win. "Don't you come in here bossing Nicki around, telling her what to do with her baby when you ain't been here."

"Ms. Jackson, Indy is my baby too, and I—"

"Boy, your mama wrote one check for that child when she was born, and we haven't seen a darn penny since. Not even a box of Pampers from none of y'all," she snapped, cutting me off. "So don't you waltz in here playing daddy whenever it's convenient for you. You men are all the same."

"I was just—"

"Save it." She threw up a hand. "Do you have any idea what it's been like for Nicki, raising Indy by herself? She's in college too, in case you forgot. She's taking classes at UDC. Got homework, a part-time job, and a baby she raises mostly alone since I work long hours."

"I'm sure it's been hard," I forced my voice to stay calm and respectful.

"Nicki had dreams," Ms. Jackson continued. "She wanted to be a singer. But no, you just had to go and knock her up."

I focused on Indy instead, on the rise and fall of her tiny chest as she finally drifted back to sleep, peaceful and unaware of the storm raging over her head. But her grandmother wasn't done.

"And don't think being gay is gonna make this any easier for that baby," she said coldly. "You need to think about the example you're setting. That poor child's gonna grow up confused. How's it gonna look when she sees you kissing a man one minute and a woman the next? Ever think about that?"

The words sliced straight through me. I couldn't believe she'd say that, and I couldn't believe she thought it. Still, I sat there like a child being scolded. Held my baby tighter as my heart began to break in front of everyone.

"You are Daddy's princess," I whispered to Indy. Her tiny infant hand gripped my pointy finger, and I felt like somewhere inside of her, she might have understood. Looking at her made me feel guilty for not being there, especially learning now that she had been sick. Poor thing was probably running a fever while I was tossing dollars at the strip club with Raven.

I looked up at Ms. Jackson, hoping she would stop her rant and go back into the kitchen, but she stood over me stony-faced with a heart cold as ice and kept going.

"...and I heard you and the Rhythm Rock Boys finally won at the Apollo," she said. "How much money you win for that contest, huh?"

"We had to split it five ways and after taxes, I paid for my schoolbooks," I lied. It was partially true. My mother had set up a college fund when they'd won the civil suit for Champ's death. I didn't have to pay for anything regarding school tuition, but the books I did. I'd blown the rest of the prize money on clothes and partying with Raven and our friends.

"You could have still given your daughter something, even a nickel, but you didn't. You are selfish and trifling is what you are!" Ms. Jackson stormed off into the kitchen, mumbling obscenities under her breath.

"I didn't know Indy was sick," I said.

"If you were here, you would know," Nicki rolled her eyes. "I can't handle this alone anymore. You'll get a child support subpoena soon."

"Child support?" I lowered my voice as Indy whimpered. "Why?"

Nicki shrugged, her eyes sliding away from mine. "What else am I supposed to do?"

I didn't need her to say it. I already knew whose idea it was.

"Fine." I handed Indy back to her and shot up from the couch.

"You're just gonna leave?" Nicki's expression hardened.

"Yeah," I snapped, reaching for my coat. "Before I say something I can't take back."

"You better not miss a payment or they'll lock you up!" Ms. Jackson yelled from the kitchen.

That did it.

I stormed in, hands clenched so tight my nails dug into my palms. For a split second her eyes widened, then she laughed.

"What do you think you're gonna do to me, little boy? Hit me?" She shook her head, amused, fat swinging from her arm as she turned the chicken in the pan. "Wouldn't be the first time a man hit me. Ask Nicki why her daddy Juan only got three fingers left on his right hand." She smirked. "Humph, I wish a nigga would."

My chest burned with anger. I spun on my heel and hurried out the door before I did something I couldn't undo.

Outside, the cold slapped me hard, but it didn't cool the fire in my chest. I was shaking from anger, scared, and I felt boxed in.

Child support. Court. Money I didn't have. How was I supposed to pay for all this? Was my dad right? Was it time to swallow my pride and flip burgers just to stay afloat? I stood there with my keys dangling from my fingers, heart racing, and mind spiraling. Staring at the scratches on my car before I stepped in.

I loved my daughter. That part was easy. Everything else felt complicated, tangled, and urgent. I had no clue what I was supposed to do next.

EIGHTEEN

Moth to a Flame

RAVEN

Scorpio was late again. Not dramatically, but enough that I almost went upstairs to my room to undress and reset my expectations. I gave him directions to my parent's house where I stayed whenever school was out for break, like now that it's spring break in April. I thought it would be easy to find, but maybe I should've just stayed with Grams in DC. Couldn't understand what was taking him so long, but then…he showed up. This was our fourth date, and we've been having a blast for two months straight!

Scorpio extended a bouquet of roses. Bloodred, impossibly fresh, like they'd just been snatched from someone's enchanted garden. And just like that, I forgave him. Not because I was easily impressed by flowers, but I found him intriguing. I loved the mystery of him.

"You look fly as always," he said, New York accent heavy, where every vowel sounded more rounded and rhythmic. Like the way he said *always* sounded more like *aw-ways.*

"You clean up pretty well yourself," I gave him a once-over. He was wearing a short-sleeved party shirt, slacks, and nice, shiny shoes. I wasn't sure where he was taking me tonight, but he told me to wear something sexy. I knew I looked good in my short fuchsia dress that stopped mid-thigh to elongate my legs. My pointy five-inch heels made us stand at almost the same height.

Our first few dates included dinner, a movie, and a concert to see Teddy Riley and Blackstreet.

"Raven, do you have your keys?" Mom asked, stepping into the foyer from the living room. My baby brother Jared, who was three, clung to her pinky finger, glancing up at me with a look that seemed to ask *Well, do you?*

"Of course," I muttered. Her eyes landed on Scorpio. I introduced them.

"Nice to meet you," Scorpio said, kissing her hand with slow deliberation. "I see where Raven gets her beauty." Loved the way he said "her" like *haw.*

Mom's cheeks flushed. She tucked a strand of hair behind her ear, lingering a second too long in his gaze for my liking.

I cleared my throat. "We need to go."

Catching my irritated look, Mom stepped back.

"Well, you kids have a nice time," she said it like I was in high school or something. I rolled my eyes as we headed out.

Scorpio opened the door to his Mercedes. He often rotated between his truck and his Benz. Who knows what other car he was going to buy next.

"We hittin' the pool hall first."

"The pool hall?" I repeated as we pulled off. I waited for him to laugh, but he didn't. He drove like he knew exactly where he was going. He wasn't joking at all. I leaned back, wondering if I was overdressed or if I was exactly the kind of girl he thought could belong anywhere.

THE POOL HALL smelled like beer, chalk, and cigars. All way too pungent and immediately erasing my perfume, leaving me to think about which cleaners I'd have to put my dress in after this. Guys in printed tees and blue jeans hunched over green tables, and Gang Starr's "Mass Appeal" pulsed low from a busted-looking speaker in the corner. Scorpio scanned the room, still holding my hand like a bodyguard. I loved feeling protected by him.

"Yo, Rodney around?" Scorpio asked one of the guys.

A man jerked a thumb toward the bar. "Over there."

"Wait here." Scorpio released my hand as I waited by the door.

I watched, curious and cautious, as Scorpio strolled over to the bar. The man sitting there, assumably Rodney, looked older. Maybe forty-something with a full beard. Two other guys were next to him, and they seemed to be laughing and joking, but stopped when they saw Scorpio approaching. They looked startled, even. Whatever Rodney and Scorpio said to each other, I couldn't hear because of everything else going on. I only saw the moment shift.

Rodney stood up quickly from the barstool, as if something Scorpio said had offended him. He was a bigger guy, too. More of a burly man with broad shoulders. Scorpio, though over six feet tall, was slim. Yet that didn't seem to faze Scorpio, who looked uncomfortable with the way Rodney stepped in his face. His brows knit together in a narrow line, and his cheek muscles taut, as if he was holding back what he really wanted to say. There was a coolness in his stare, but beneath it, a hint of irritation flickered across his expression. Next thing I knew, he punched Rodney so hard the sound made me cringe and look away. When I glanced back, Rodney lay unconscious on the wooden floor.

Scorpio leaned down, reached into Rodney's pants pocket, and pulled out a fat roll of cash.

The bartender looked away, pretending to be busy cleaning glasses. The other guys lifted Rodney off the floor but didn't go after Scorpio. They looked too scared to intervene.

Scorpio walked over to me, smiling like it was nothing.

"Ready to go, babe?" It wasn't a question. He was already pulling me by the hand.

Out the door we went. My breath caught halfway between fear and fascination as I walked alongside Scorpio with his calm swagger.

"May I ask what Rodney did to warrant your response?" I

inquired once we were outside, speaking more quietly than usual. While somewhat apprehensive, my curiosity remained genuine.

"He disrespected me. Took me for a sucker by not paying me what he owed." Scorpio gritted his teeth. Then, with a grin that could melt a stack of bricks, he asked, "You like reggae music?"

"Uh, yeah. Sure."

"Good. We're going to the Kilimanjaro."

PATRA WAS PERFORMING her hit "Worker Man" from the stage, letting all the women in the club know that she had a real man problem because men like to play games. Scorpio held my hand as we zigzagged through the crowd and found our way to the VIP table near the back. The air smelled like spice, jerk chicken, and marijuana. My stomach growled, I was hungry.

Scorpio moved like he owned the place. Everyone knew him. Dapped him up, gave him nods of respect. I was the girl on his arm. The one in a world I'd only ever seen from a safe suburban distance. And I liked the way it felt. It was different from Dawson, whose popularity didn't come with this rebellious danger that always left me curious as to what was going to happen next. With Dawson, and other guys I'd dated just like him, life was predictable.

Scorpio pulled the chair for me to sit down. A waitress asked him if he was having his usual, and he nodded. She turned to ask me what I was having but didn't ask for my ID or payment.

"Long Island Iced Tea," I said confidently. I wasn't old enough to drink yet, but it wouldn't be my first time getting away with having a drink at a club, let's be honest.

"You always bring girls here?" I asked, letting the straw tap against my lip after the waitress brought our drinks a few minutes later. Scorpio swallowed a Kamikaze shot.

He looked at me, eyes half-lidded, as we sat across from each other at a small round table.

"No."

That was it. No explanation. No extra words. Just… no. Like always, his answers were short.

"So, I'm special?"

"Didn't say all that either."

I laughed, tipping my head back, more amused than offended. "Gosh, you're so freakin' annoying."

He watched me closely. "And you like it."

I did.

"So, I've been meaning to ask, what's your real name?"

"Scorpio."

I rolled my eyes. "You're impossible."

"You're nosy."

"I'm curious."

"Same thing," he said, as his eyes seemed to follow something or someone behind me. That's when I felt a tap on my shoulder.

"Rave, what're you doing here?"

"Lucci, I should be asking you that. Like, aren't you supposed to be in New York?"

"I was. I came home this weekend to see my sons. Leaving town tomorrow. Just here celebrating with da homies since Midtown signed me."

"Congrats Cuz! That is so awesome!" I beamed. "Well, let me introduce you. This is Scorpio. Scorpio this is my cousin, Lucci."

Lucci's eyes cut to Scorpio the second I introduced them, and the shift was instant. It was like the music dulled, the lights dimmed, and the whole club leaned in to watch. Scorpio didn't smile. Didn't move. He just leaned back in his chair, sizing Lucci up with that cold, steady stare that made men think twice before breathing wrong.

Lucci didn't flinch either. His shoulders squared, and the muscles in his face tightened like he was daring Scorpio to blink first. The tension was immediate, like two storms colliding in silence.

Lucci's voice cut sharp. "Why you messing with this bama nigga?"

"Excuse me?" I propped a hand on my hip. "You're being rude, Lucci."

"Come on, get away from this dude right now." Lucci grabbed my arm and jerked me up from the chair. Pulled me away.

"Lucci, stop! What're you doing?"

He pulled me aside. "You don't need to be messing with Scorpio. You're out of your league with this one, Cuz. For real."

"Now you sound like Boogie."

"Then listen to us. Scorpio ain't the type to put your heels in the air for."

"You don't tell me what to do!"

"Leave him alone, Raven, for real. If you don't, it's gonna be a tombstone with your name on it."

I yanked my arm from his grip. "We're just having fun. You're making this a big deal."

"Hate being a rat, but since I won't be around, I'm telling Uncle Raymond. If you won't listen to me, you will listen to your father."

"I'm grown. A sophomore in college, in case you forgot."

"Cuz, I'm dead serious. Leave. Scorpio. Alone." His brown eyes locked onto mine.

"Like I said, I'm grown. Good luck in New York."

"Blood over water, Cuz." Lucci stared at me without blinking. "You must've forgot."

"That doesn't apply to this situation. Not this time."

Lucci shook his head, then walked off with his friends.

Back at the table, Scorpio was talking to someone on his cellphone as I sat back down across from him.

"...no problem. It's handled," he was saying before hanging up.

"I'm sorry for what happened just now. My cousin Lucci was just being protective of me."

"He's jealous that I'm the man he was never fit to be is all."

"What's that supposed to mean?"

"Turk made me his right-hand man. I had to come down from New York to fix what little niggas like Lucci messed up."

I blinked in shock. Surprised he had told me that much.

"You're lucky I like you enough not to put your cousin on a stretcher."

I stared at him for a second, his words hit heavier than the music. Still, I whispered, "Lucci's just looking out for me."

He choked back another shot glass before he spoke again. "You don't need him or nobody else. What I say goes and what I do backs it up. As long as you with me, ain't nobody gonna bother you. Word is bond."

I felt myself smiling on the inside at the way he said he'd protect me. Surely, he wouldn't hurt me since he cared more about keeping me protected, right? Lucci and Boogie had him all wrong.

"You want to dance?" I asked, trying to lighten the mood.

"I don't dance. I watch. Go do your thing."

I slipped away to the dance floor. Spotted Lucci with his friends dancing with some girls. Lucci happened to look up while I was dancing and shook his head, disgusted with me. Maybe he was jealous of Scorpio after all. A lot of guys were. He was young, only twenty-seven I'd learned, and making a lot of money.

Scorpio leaned back and watched me dance to a few songs, but not for long. The second another guy got too close, he was at my back, arms around my hips, claiming me to the rhythm of Bob Marley's "Is This Love."

"Thought you'd see it my way," I teased, turning back to him as he wrapped his long arms around the curves of my hips. Heat crawled up my neck with each touch of his hands sliding over my body. I hate how much he makes me like him, knowing how dangerous he is. I'm trying not to fall too hard.

We locked eyes without blinking. The bass rolled beneath our feet like thunder as we swayed off rhythm, clumsy even. He had two left feet, but when he pulled me close, I didn't want him to let go. I wanted our slow island sway to erase the dark edges of tonight.

He hummed the lyrics softly in my ear with his cheek warm against mine. The scent of liquor and a hint of cologne drifted from his skin but underneath lingered something wild and raw. Something totally reckless that seemed to carry the night itself. And I loved it.

I moved with the music, arms around his neck, letting myself sink into him, pushing thoughts of Lucci and Boogie's warnings far from my mind. When his body shifted against mine, the rhythm turned flirtier. I couldn't resist.

"Kiss me," I whispered.

He didn't hesitate. His mouth claimed mine, the kiss long and deep, all heat, hunger, and liquor-sweet tongue. When we finally pulled apart, he wiped lipstick from his mouth. Some of it smeared on his shirt.

He slid both hands over my curves, gripping me just enough to make me catch my breath. "Let's get outta here."

SCORPIO and I ended up at Hains Point, his car angled just enough toward the water where you could see the city lights glittering across the Potomac.

Inside the car, the dashboard glowed low as the radio played Silk's "Lose Control," barely louder than our kissing. His hand traveled up my thigh and paused, like he was testing how far I wanted him to go. I parted my legs to give him permission to divide and conquer me in any way he desired.

Every kiss left a mark I could feel even after his mouth moved to the next part of my body. We kissed until we worked up a heat that fogged the windows, blurring the Washington Monument and the Capitol until the world looked like a faint background in a portrait.

Somehow, we ended up in the backseat. Knees knocking, bodies fitting where they technically shouldn't, laughter breaking once or twice until we figured out how to mesh together in the backseat. His jacket slipped off, my skirt rode higher as movements and tongues flickered with intensity. Every touch answered the last. The leather creaked beneath us as the car rocked hard enough to draw attention and feel like a motion ride. We rocked and rocked until the moment heightened as we braced for the big wave, hollering in pure ecstasy as it came to a simultaneous slow *Ohhhh* and pulsating end.

My legs loosened as Scorpio leaned his forehead against mine and tried to catch his breath. The windshield was completely fogged now, opaque and protective, as if the night had politely turned its back. We stayed like that, saying nothing. The radio played another slow jam by an artist I forgot and didn't care to remember. Scorpio shifted, trying to stretch his long legs forward, cramped and smiling like he didn't mind one bit. We exchanged kisses, gradually feeling a heat rise again. I didn't want the night to end just yet, so I lured him back on top of me, but then—

Headlights swept across the car, bright and sudden. We stopped. Craned our necks and spotted a park patrol cruiser rolling by. We scrambled to fix our clothes before it could circle back, then we slipped into the front seats and pulled away as if we'd been doing nothing at all. We laughed like teenagers with our adrenaline running from the thrill of not getting caught.

A few minutes passed, and we settled down, watching the sky give way to first hints of dawn with streaks of light stretching over the city as the darkness slowly gave way. As we cruised down the highway, Scorpio glanced at me. His eyes looked soft and steady, stripped of bravado, as if the chaos of the night had finally melted into stillness. When we came upon a red light, after exiting the highway, he turned toward me.

"Remember when you asked my real name?"

"Yes," I blushed, taking hold of his free hand, intertwining my fingers between his.

"It's Ivan," he said with a half-grin like he was finally surrendering. "Ivan Jakes."

I squeezed his hand, feeling the warmth of a new beginning stir between us. He was my man, and I was his woman. A quiet sense of hope settled in my heart, promising that whatever came next, we'd face it together.

NINETEEN

Night Catches Us

SCORPIO

The house was dark when I pulled up to my spot in Bowie, Maryland, bout twenty minutes outside of DC. I don't ever work where I sleep. No way I'm lettin' the grime from the hoods I hustle in touch my family, know what I'm saying? Normally, Simone leaves the kitchen light or the dimmers low in the living room, but as I parked in the driveway, not a single light spilled through the windows. No familiar glow, just blackness behind the sheer curtains. An indication that she didn't wait up for me, at least not this time. It was almost four in the morning.

I cut the engine and sat there for a minute. I tried to think of an excuse for not coming home earlier. Raven's sweet and warm perfume stuck to my shirt like it was made that way. Her liquor breath still on my lips, too. Shorty was cute, curious, and bold. She got her own bag and don't need mine. And she fine! Man, she's a straight banger! Never met a chick as pretty as her before in my whole life. I'm trying not to fall for her, but she may have to move from a side piece to my main queen.

I should've drove straight home after the club, but Raven kept kissin' on me, grinding against me, and talkin' slick, so yeah, I caved in. I shook shorty out her skin and had her shaking like a caterpillar.

But right now? I need another excuse for Simone. I was runnin' low. Started with ducking marrying her like I promised when she got pregnant with our son and then our daughter a year later. Two kids, back-to-back, they five and four. Got her a bigger ring, made her a bigger promise, and moved her down here from Harlem. I did all that, you know what I'm saying? Tried to be a good family man or whatever, but temptation is a trip. It's my weak spot, can't lie. Women love me. It's like I got gravity in my skin.

I unlocked the front door real slowly, easing it shut so the hinges wouldn't snap too loud. I crept up the stairs, trying to avoid the areas I knew would make a loud squeaking noise.

"You think I don't hear you?" Simone's low, husky voice slid through the darkness.

I exhaled heavily. *Busted!*

She hit the lights. Suddenly, everything lit up bright and made me feel more exposed.

"Don't ever come out the dark like that," I said, making myself the victim.

"Where you been, Ivan?" She propped one hand on her hip.

"Simone, go ahead with that. Chill out. It's late," I hissed, not wanting to wake up our kids with another night of us arguing and whatnot.

"No, it's early." Simone followed me up the stairs and down the hall into our bedroom, anger hot in her tone. "Past four in the morning early. *Again*!"

"I told you I had to handle some business tonight."

"Business don't leave lipstick on your shirt and reeking perfume."

I looked down. Raven's red lipstick sat on the fabric like a signature. *Rookie mistake. Sloppy. Gotta do better.*

"Don't start with me, Simone," I said, kicking off my shoes. Trying to twist this crap on her as best I could.

Her green eyes sliced through me. "Nigga, what? You walkin' up in here wet, smellin' like some other chick, and I'm just supposed to sit pretty and smile?"

“Can we just… go to sleep?” I tossed my shirt inside the hamper in the closet. The second I shut it, Simone got even louder.

“Sleep?” she barked, light face turning red. “I been up all night losing my mind! Thinking you got smoked or worse. So, what happened this time? Huh? Some girl trip and fall onto your lap? Or did you crawl into hers?”

“Enough!” I grabbed her cheeks with one hand, pressing my fingers hard into her jawline. “The questions stop right now. I don’t want to hear anymore. Cuz you lucky I still come home.” I turned her loose. “Be glad of that.”

Her chin shook. She knew not to say nothin’ else. She was outta pocket talking to me like I wasn’t the man of my own house. I pay all the bills and call the shots in this joint.

I brushed past her, grabbed a towel and washcloth out the linen closet. Guilt nipped at my heels, but Raven’s laugh still echoed in my head. She danced like she was queen of the club tonight. Reminded me of Simone when we still lived in Harlem. First night I saw her, she was beautiful, swinging them short thick legs around that pole. I fell for her fast. That was five years ago. But that shine and beauty drowned in diapers, formula, and bills real quick. Left me working three jobs trying to feed my babies. Then big Cuzzo Turk pulled up with a brick and a promise.

“Move this. You do good, there’s more,” he told me, and I never looked back since.

I slid into bed after a shower and noticed Simone wasn’t there, but the engagement ring I gave her was sitting on the nightstand under the lamp. As soon as I spotted it, I heard the guest room door down the hall slam shut. This wasn’t over. Not even close.

I made a mental note to call my homey Rob’s sister tomorrow. Roberta’s a travel agent. Gonna see if she can book a cruise for me and Simone. She’ll be wearing my ring again soon. She don’t get to say it’s over. I do.

TWENTY

Fame: What You Like Is the Limo

LUCCI

Spring 1994

Backstage at BET's *Rap City* in DC, Bone Thugz N' Harmony's "Thuggish Ruggish Bone" played on the big TV, distracting me from remembering my lyrics. Couldn't turn it off because everyone in the green room was listening to it. I donned my headphones and hit the play button on my Discman. Needing to hear my own song and feel the beat, I took a breath, adjusted my thick chain with its L-shaped platinum diamond pendant, and paced the room as I rapped.

Muttering my lyrics, I wore a red hoodie with my microphone logo, FUBU shorts, and new kicks. Even with my look together, nerves hit before my first televised show. Now signed to Midtown Records, I needed to prove I was worthy of the three-album deal and $300K advance.

"Lucci, ready?"

I turned to see Chaundra, the makeup artist. Pausing my Discman, I went to her booth, where she quickly brushed my cheekbones. The mirror showed my tense expression.

"Close your eyes," she said as she finished up. She smiled, reaching for eyeliner. "Almost done."

"I'm good," I said, raising my hand.

"But—"

"For real, save the liner for a rock star."

Rasheeda, known to everyone as "Rah," stepped into the room with the confidence of someone in charge, her sweet, perfumed oil announcing her arrival even before she appeared. Though I'd crossed paths with her in New York, our interactions had been nothing more than a casual "wassup" in passing.

Rah was a fly, bowlegged Jamaican queen, thick in all the right places, and her energy was magnetic. In the industry, she was already legend in the hairstyle game, especially with braids. If you wanted your corners tight and your edges slicked back with no frizz, Rah was the one who had you looking like that.

"Mon, yu shoulda let me braid em hair first 'fore yu start em makeup," Rah shouted at Chaundra, her Jamaican accent heavy. I loved it. Her own hair was styled in microbraids and pulled into a high ponytail, slick baby hairs all even around her hairline. She looked cute.

"I have other clients to get to before it's showtime," Chaundra explained.

"Butcha wreckin' me flow." Rah stared her down. "What if him sweat? Ya tink about dat? Him gon sit in me chair a while, mon. Makeup may run down. Den what? Yu gon do again?"

My eyes bounced between the two of them, waiting for some *Jerry Springer Show* type of action to go down. You know, a catfight joint.

Chaundra's eyes darted every which way. She looked embarrassed like a mug. She ain't want that heat from Rah, for real.

"Sorry, it won't happen again," Chaundra lamented. "I'll redo his makeup if I need to."

"Yu definitely will. Him can't go on TV like bum, ya know? Fix em up." Rah walked over to her booth. I stood there unsure of what my next move should be since the room was tense between them, know what I'm saying?

Rah turned from Chaundra, smiled at me, and her cute dimple formed in her left cheek. She quickly turned off her anger and said, "Hey, superstar," in a warm voice. "Come to me chair."

I walked over and she draped her salon cape around me. Her brand logo, "Rah Locs," was on the front. I took notes at how everyone was trying to brand themselves.

"Let's getcha lookin' sharp, eh. Ready for ya TV debut. Ya thinkin cornrows straight back or wit dah zigzag parts, mon?"

I shrugged. "Don't matter to me. As long as I look good and I'm not late, know what I'm saying?" I licked my lips.

She nodded. "Me like dat. Keep on time, mon. When dem celebs blow up, dem forget how dem should treat peoples, ya know."

"I'll try not to be like that."

She winked and went to pull out her tools: a rattail comb, Blue Magic hair grease, and brown gel. She worked her fingers fast and skillfully. Figured Rah was probably about twenty-five, but she acted like she was thirty-something the way she commanded the room.

"Relax, mon. Me can feel the tension in yu scalp. Ya got this," she said in a motherly tone.

"Dang, how you know how I'm feeling right now?" I puckered my brow, glanced at her before the mirror in front of us.

"Been doin' hair since me was a lil girl, ya know. A woman knows dese tings. Just chill, boo. It is okay, eh."

I exhaled, wiped my sweaty hands on the front of my shorts. "I'm trying to."

She spun me around in the chair and looked me dead in the eyes. "Trust me, some peoples come through dem doors a one-hit-wonder, but not yu. When you rap, me can hear every emotion, mon. Me feel yu pain 'bout ya struggle. People gonna love you, mon. Dis won't be yu last rodeo ride, no. Yu watch and ya see."

I nodded, trying to believe her words, but my anxiety was giving me bubble guts.

When Rah finished braiding my hair in zigzag-style braids, the sweet smell of Blue Magic hair grease lingered in the air, and my scalp tingled where her nimble fingers had worked their skills. She sprayed my head with oil sheen for the finishing touch.

"Thanks."

"Any time." Rah winked.

I proceeded to the hallway to call G-Ma so we could talk without folks in my business.

The hallway outside the dressing room was a blur of movement. The stagehands hustled past with headsets and clipboards, a stylist pushed a rack of clothes on wheels, someone carried a tray of drinks, and voices echoed in bursts and last-minute pep talks and whatnot. My kicks squeaked against the polished linoleum as I found a corner down the stretch of the hall. Dialed with my sweaty fingers slipping a little.

"Hey G-Ma," I said, my throat feeling tight, trying not to let my nerves show.

"Lucci, I'm trying to find you on the TV right now. What channel is it?" G-Ma asked, her voice booming with the kind of raspy warmth that always made me feel at home. G-Ma had seen and lived through plenty yet still managed to wrap every word in humor and affection.

"We gotta tape it first. I'm on set now." My heartbeat thudded in my chest, and I could feel the sweat falling from my temples. "When I'm done, I'm gonna come and see you. BET right over here in Brentwood off Rhode Island Avenue."

"Child, you know I don't know anything about no doggone BET, but I do remember *Soul Train*," she chuckled, her laughter rich and nostalgic.

"Yeah…figured that, but it's all good." I switched ears as a makeup artist darted by, pushing a cart of cosmetics.

"You go out there and give them a show. Make us all proud, baby." Her words wrapped around me like a soft quilt, and the excitement in her voice helped to build my confidence.

"You deserve the big stage after all you done been through, son. Even your dad called and said he can't wait to see you perform. Go out there and show them what you're made of. You're a Walker. You can do it!"

Her words washed over me like a calm lavender soap, and some of the tension eased from my shoulders. I don't know how she sensed I was nervous.

"Thanks, G-Ma." I hung up the phone, and when I turned around, Rah was standing behind me with her arms spread open.

"Ya look like ya need a hug, mon."

I leaned down. We embraced. I unconsciously let my hands drop low to squeeze that sexy apple bottom. OK, I did it *consciously*.

"Keep calm, mon." She pushed my hands back but blushed a little. "We friends. Dat tis all."

"For now." My eyes swayed with hers.

"Let's roll, guys, it's showtime in ten seconds!" the stage manager shouted, running through the studio backstage with a head-mic around his head.

"Catch you later," I told Rah and followed the stage manager toward the set.

With my new confidence on lock, I stepped up with my swag on when they dropped my name. Crowd roarin', lights flashing, everybody vibin' to my new track, "Still Standing," over a sample by Juicy's "Sugar Free." I started spitting bars over the beat, memories flashed from when I was wreckin' freestyle battles at Neat Plains Juvenile in Ohio. Now I'm live on BET's *Rap City*. Man, this is next-level, can't believe it's real!

I grew up in a storm that I ain't choose
Mama noddin' off and her arms was bruised,
refrigerator empty, roaches everywhere,
learned early on that life wasn't fair

Wakin' up to sirens, neighbors fightin' in the streets,
Hand-me-down dreams, and busted up sneaks
While the block slept, I was out with rags,
Bucket full of soap, washin' cars for cash

But I rose from the dirt, turned pain into pride,
Even when my mother left me stranded outside.
Survivor since birth, you can see my scars,

I came up from nothin' now I'm one of the stars.

I'm still standing…

AFTER MY PERFORMANCE ON BET, the phones at Midtown were ringing off the hook. In less than a month, I was on the cover of *The Source Magazine-Lucci Loot, A Hit Making DC Underdog.* Sent a copy to G-Ma and she framed it. I was on my way to the big time!

TWENTY-ONE

Sorry Can't Fix It

IRENE

I knew Diane was coming before the door opened. Her perfume entered the room first, soft, expensive, and floral in a way that pretended innocence. It didn't belong here. It slid through the hospital's ammonia-heavy air, bringing a scent of freshness that seemed to belong only outside. I pressed my fingertips into my thighs as my palms began to sweat. I tried to keep myself grounded. Silence had always been safer. Silence never surprised me.

Diane stepped in wearing the smell of a life that was still moving forward. She wore a linen pantsuit. Her hair was styled in long curls that flowed down her back deliberately. She carried a leather briefcase like proof she'd come from somewhere important. Court perhaps. Her eyes swept the room quickly as if she wanted to ensure her safety before the guard took duty at the farthest corner of the room.

She sat down slowly across the table, placing her briefcase at her high-heeled feet. She looked smaller than I remembered. Her eyes were still big, beautiful but cautious. This room didn't bend to her the way courtrooms and offices probably did. Her perfume bloomed as she moved closer, scooting her chair to the table so she could place her hands down. Her perfectly manicured hands look like she had a maid who probably did all the work. Growing up, I did both our chores while Diane was always conveniently sick when it came time to do house chores.

My breath shortened with anxiety. We hadn't been face-to-face like this in decades. Both in our forties now, and we'd only seen each other in passing at Mama's house. Mostly her passing me. She avoided me at every chance she had, and never once came to visit me as I wasted away upstairs in the bedroom. Nor had she come to visit since I'd been hospitalized.

Silence pooled between us with the clicking clock on the wall as the only sound. I looked down, twiddled my thumbs under the table, and prayed silently for the strength to push through this moment.

She cleared her throat. "Hello, Irene."

I lifted my gaze slowly.

"I wasn't sure you'd want to see me," she said. "Raven thought it might help."

So even now, you couldn't see a point in visiting your own sister without being convinced? I thought to myself as the memories flashed through my mind of us whispering under blankets as little girls. Diane would squeeze my hand and yell that she was afraid of the Boogeyman, and me promising I'd protect her from the monster. I never expected that years later, I'd be the one needing protection from a real-life one. The anger inside me didn't explode from the memories, but it settled. Low and hot like a pot on the stove. Maybe the meds were keeping me calm, at least for now.

"I never wanted this for you," she said quickly, as if my facial expression looked like a threat. Maybe it was the way I winced my eyes at her as she spoke.

"Percy Knight, I thought he was safe. He was smart like you and stayed to himself. I thought you would like someone like him and vice versa."

Well, you were wrong! I thought, clenching my teeth.

"I've carried that guilt for years." Her voice cracked. Whether it was real or rehearsed, I couldn't tell. Not yet. But she has the nerve to say she carried guilt.

Carried? As if the pain of what I had experienced hadn't been strapped to *my* back instead.

"I was jealous of you."

There it was. Not an apology. An explanation, like always.

"You were everything," she said. "The smart one. Teachers loved you. Mom and Dad"—her voice wavered—"they bragged about you. I wanted that. I wanted to be you, Irene."

Tears filled her eyes slowly, carefully, as if she were measuring how much emotion the room would allow without rejecting her. Suddenly, she stood and then walked around the table to me.

My body reacted before my thoughts could catch up. She wrapped her arms around me, and I flinched at first, then my muscles stalled. Froze me. I didn't move, but inside, something screamed as she held me anyway. Her arms were warm and familiar but felt wrong. *Is she sincere?*

"I never came before because it hurt too much," she sobbed. "Seeing you like this—"

Like this? As if I were the Beast in *Beauty in the Beast.* A human turned into an animal attraction.

"Please," she whispered. "Say something. I'd do anything to hear your voice again."

She pulled back and searched my face for something absolute. For permission perhaps. I didn't respond. Didn't know how. Not yet.

I watched her as she sat back down in the seat across from me, like she'd given up hope. Her shoulders slumped, her eyes clouded, and her gaze drifted downward, unable to meet mine for more than a second.

And then something inside me cracked open.

"Diane…"

Her eyes flew wide open.

My rusty voice even scared me when I heard it. It had been unused for nearly twenty-two years. The sound hit the room like glass shattering, making Diane jolt. She jerked back in the chair like she'd seen a ghost, and the color drained from her face.

"You… you just—" she gasped. "You spoke."

"Yes." My voice trembled, then steadied. "You don't know what I lost because of what happened."

She held my gaze like she was trying to figure out if it was me who was really talking.

"I didn't just lose my body that night," I admitted. "I lost my life."

She looked away momentarily. I didn't know if she felt guilty or embarrassed, but I couldn't stop now. Pent-up emotions bubbled forth that couldn't be written down. The words needed to be said.

"I didn't get to finish college like you. My dreams of becoming a teacher or anything else died on that night," I continued. "My daughter grew up without me. I missed her milestones, couldn't guide her, couldn't protect her. I was just a shadow in the distance. Mama had to raise her for me."

Her breath hitched, a hand came to her mouth like this was the first time she knew this. She always knew, but I guess hearing it hit differently.

"And worst of all, I had no voice to tell my daughter the truth," I went on. "Does she even know? Because I never saw him come around."

Diane's eyebrows wrinkled a puzzled expression.

"About Evan Graham," I stated.

Confusion crossed her face. Then a realization. A truth she knew but maybe buried it along with forgetting about me.

"She doesn't know, does she?" I pressed.

Diane's lips parted in thought.

I lifted my hand to stop her from thinking of another excuse. "Don't explain. Now that I have my voice back, I'll decide when she finds out. Not you."

"But I—"

"No, it's my turn to talk. It's your business to listen now," I reminded her firmly without raising my voice. "You weren't the only one *carrying* any of this all these years. While you were busy building your life with Raymond, Raven's father, I was disappearing. When you were rising as a top lawyer, I was hidden. You got forward motion, but I got stuck, and our brother Donovan? He got years in prison."

My chest tightened as feelings heated from the pit of my stomach. "My daughter left me," I choked, swallowing down tears. "And I couldn't even say goodbye before she went off to college."

The guard, sensing tension, moved closer toward us.

"What do I have left, Diane?" I asked, blood boiling now. I couldn't control it any longer. "Tell me!" I slammed my hand against the table, causing her to jerk in shock.

She blinked in startled panic. Looked around like she hoped someone else would rescue her with a lawyer-like rebuttal. There wasn't anyone. Not Mama. Not Daddy. Just the guard, four walls, and a TV playing *Melrose Place* from the wall without volume.

"You came here out of pity, didn't you?" I asked, voice sharper around the edges. "You want my forgiveness, but you don't get to hurt me and decide when I'm done bleeding,"

"I—I'm sorry," she cried.

"Yes. You are. And you can take sorry right out that door with you."

Shock cracked across her face. It was raw and almost childlike. She hadn't prepared for this version of me. She'd been used to the quiet and accommodating person I used to be, but that version of me died on that floor when she was violated. The woman sitting across from her now was courageous and stood on her truth. Determined not to settle for people's crap anymore.

The guard stepped forward and held out a tissue. Diane took it without looking at him, without a thank you. She sat there, shoulders stiff, breathing unevenly, staring at nothing as though she were trying to absorb what my words meant. When she finally moved, her gaze landed on her briefcase. She reached for it. The guard reacted instantly, crossing the room in two quick strides.

"It's just a gift," she said hoarsely, irritation flashing beneath the tears.

The guard hesitated, then stepped back.

Diane opened the briefcase and pulled out a framed photograph, small and careful, as if it were fragile. "This is for you. I had it on my office desk ever since I finished law school. It got me through."

She extended it to me, and I took it gently into my hand feeling unsure of what kind of picture it was until I looked at it. My breath instantly caught in my throat. *Wow! She kept this?*

The photo showed us as little girls, barefoot in the living room, frozen in a moment before life learned how to split us apart. Diane had her arm hooked around my shoulders, hugging me from the side. My flower crown sat crooked, slipping over one eye. Our father had taken the picture with a Polaroid camera. The colors were soft and faded, but clear enough to let me know Diane had it reprinted professionally and enlarged.

I pressed the photograph to my chest, and the anger loosened its grip as my mind slipped backward in time. Glue had dried on our fingertips that day. Mama always kept us busy with arts and crafts, determined to give us something pure to hold on to. In those moments, I was the queen and Diane the princess, rulers of a make-believe world where nothing bad ever happened. It was our wonderful imaginations that made me believe I could be a good elementary school teacher.

That was when the anger dissolved into sorrow, and the tears came. Not because forgiveness had arrived, but after decades of silence, I remembered what joy felt like before it was stolen and sealed away with my voice.

When I opened my eyes, Diane was gone. The door had closed behind her with a soft click. Through the narrow glass window, I watched another guard escort her down the hall toward the exit. I knew then that I couldn't remain angry forever. But something unfamiliar stirred in me. Something fragile enough to make me feel nervous. It was the possibility of a new life beyond these walls. One that Ms. Lanham promised once Diane and I had finally talked, and I'd found my voice again.

Hope barely had time to settle before the room cast a shadow. The two little girls took shape slowly, as if my mind needed time to admit them. They stood near the door, holding hands—one in a red dress, the other in black. They had never held hands before. They didn't move. They didn't speak this time. They only looked at me, as if waiting.

My thoughts trembled. *Would I ever be free from what Diane started? Would I ever be able to live a life peacefully after the damage Percy Knight had caused? Would I ever love a man again?*

As if hearing the questions, the girls turned toward each other. Their grips tightened around each other's hands. They smiled at each other without showing teeth. Without looking back, they walked through the door, holding hands until they vanished into the hall.

The room fell silent. Maybe it always was, but it felt heavier whenever they were present. The girls did not return.

I didn't know whether their leaving meant I was healed or simply alone with myself for the first time without any more hallucinations. But I understood this much: whatever future waited for me, it felt like it would no longer include them. And that, somehow, felt like both an ending and a new beginning.

TWENTY-TWO

Gigolo

BOOGIE

My friend Flava from the Rhythm Rock Boys got me into doing questionable errands for lonely grandmas with surprisingly deep pockets. I loved the money, but God had already tapped me on the shoulder about it. I just wasn't listening yet. It happened last week at church, as I sat between Grandma and Mom, and every time I glanced across the aisle, Ms. Dudley grinned at me with a pearly-white denture smile that made my soul cave in. Her son was our pastor. He was up there preaching about people living double lives and harboring secret sins. Guilt made me cry, but it wasn't enough to make me stop doing what I had been. I knew better.

Of all the grannies, I never knew Ms. Dudley was the one Flava referred until she opened the door that night. I was wearing my usual suit and tie. Ms. Dudley was a recent widow and deeply lonely. Flava had "referred" her. I hated that word now as much as I hated chest hair. She enjoyed herself so much she told all her "Bengay Betty" friends. Child, the money was *easy*. A couple glasses of wine, a boring game of Gin Rummy, and a quick slam bam, then boom—credit card and child support relief. *Cha-ching!* It kept Nicki and her mom off my back.

Still, every time I left a client's house, I'd lock myself in the bathroom like I'd committed a felony against my own soul. Scrubbing my skin until I exfoliated a new personality. I felt like I was cheating on the real me. Flava, though? Oh, honey, he slept just fine. He told me the other day, "Them scallywag widows get theirs, and I get mine."

He'd count money like Proverbs couldn't give him wisdom and a way out. His side hustle had recently expanded from grandmas to wealthy old gentlemen. I'd crossed that bridge once or twice, but I preferred my fruit ripe, not pruned. Anyway, I knew I needed to stop what I'd been doing. Yet here I am. Tonight's client is Simone.

Simone was twenty-eight with green eyes. She was about my height, short, and a little chunky, but face cute or whatever. Her hair is honey blonde like mine, except her weave flowed down her back like Lady Godiva on a hunt for chocolate. She'd learned about me through word of mouth, which honestly should've been my first warning that things were getting out of control. But the women were talking. "Mr. Nolan gets the job done," I'd even overheard them say. Nolan, my biological name that I still hated as much as what I was doing, I told them to use that so no one would confuse it with my stage name, Boogie.

Compared to my usual senior regulars though, Simone was a breeze. No menthol smell. No orthopedic shoes. No catching leg cramps. But Miss Thing had *energy*, so I charged extra for an additional hour.

She tugged at my tropical shirt while I stood at the water cooler in her kitchen, refilling a cup. We were done, but I was hot and thirsty. I needed to hydrate and flee this immoral sinkhole before it swallowed me whole.

"Dessert?" she asked, casual as sweet tea.

I shook my head no. I didn't like to linger or socialize beyond what was required. Flava warned me not to get too personal, so I kept the mystery. The less conversation, the fewer lies to remember.

Simone floated around the kitchen island, cut herself a slice of cake, while I leaned against the counter near the sink, wiping sweat from my forehead and catching my breath. My mind drifted like it always did. Maybe my life would've been different if Lucci had taken me on the road with him. But no. He didn't want other rappers knowing he had a bisexual cousin.

"At least try a little piece," Simone teased, already cutting a slice for me. "I love baking."

She didn't know I had a daughter waiting on diapers and formula. She didn't know that extra two-fifty she paid me to stay longer would cover the sitter this week.

She walked over and fed me a piece the way wedding couples do. Slow and flirty. The cake was strawberry and delicious. She stepped back, licked the extra frosting off her fingertip as she held my gaze.

"I need to go now," I said.

Just as I was about to walk out of the kitchen, that's when I saw it. Right there, taped below the calendar on the fridge. It was surrounded by fruit and butterfly magnets. The kind you buy in bulk because your kids lose them easily. Simone stood on a beach, hair blowing in the wind, and she looked slimmer. She was laughing into the bare chest of a man I recognized before my brain even caught up.

My heart immediately ran up to the altar and slid *off. No, please God, don't let it be so. No. No. NO!*

"You okay?" Simone asked. I stood there with my mouth gaped open. She followed my stare and clucked her teeth. "Oh, that picture is old. Don't worry about him. He's probably running the streets with that hoe I told you he's cheating on me with. I got mine tonight too." She said it like she was bragging. "Relax. I'm not expecting him home anytime soon if you want to go another round."

Was she stupid, dumb, or crazy? Her man was Scorpio! A known killer in these streets. Child, my spirit left my body and took the express bus home.

This was the same Scorpio my bestie-cousin had been floating around campus talking about, *"Scorpio got my heart,"* like the man was single. The picture next to the beach one was a family photo at an amusement park. Scorpio, Simone, and their two kids who were spitting images of them.

My skin began to crawl. This meant I was standing in the kitchen of the woman involved with my cousin's man. Which meant I had just slept with my cousin's man's fiancée. Which meant I had officially entered mess I could not pray, fast, or scripture-read my way out of. As my grandmother would say, *Boy, you done did it now!*

And right then, before I could shut my mouth from the shock, headlights slid across the kitchen window.

Simone stiffened so fast I thought she'd been unplugged.

"Oh no!" she hissed. "He's home early."

"What?" I panicked. "But you just said—"

"I know what I said," she snapped, rushing to the light switch. "Come on, let's get you out of here."

As she pushed me, I jammed my pager into my pocket and froze. I patted my back pocket. Then the other. Nothing.

"Wait, where's my wallet?" I whispered, pausing before leaving out the back door. "I don't have my wallet."

Simone's eyes widened. "What do you mean you don't—"

"I mean it's on that counter," I glanced back like Lot's wife.

"Boy, we don't have time for that," she shoved me. "Just go!"

"Alright, but make sure you grab it, so he won't see it and know I was here."

The cool night air slapped my skin as the door clicked shut behind me like a period at the end of the sentence. I took off toward the fence.

WOOF. WOOF. WOOF.

At first it was just sound. Then I reached the fence and saw a pack of Rottweilers slamming against a chain-link cage like it might give way. Under the alley streetlights, their eyes burned animal-gold and locked on me like raw meat. Teeth gnashed and spit flew. Honey, adrenaline did the thinking for me. Instead of unlocking the fence, I jumped it like a bank robber. My hands scraped against the metal. Halfway over, something *yanked*. I felt the rip across my back before I heard it, but I didn't dare look back. I hit the ground running. The barking followed me down the alley, echoing like they were right behind me. I ran until my lungs burned and my vision narrowed to a tunnel. I needed my inhaler. Forgot that too.

Slow down, Boogie. Breathe. I bent over with my hands on my knees, sucking air that wouldn't come, heart hammering like it wanted out. All I could see was my wallet still sitting on Simone's counter like a ticking time bomb.

God, please get me home safe and in one piece, I prayed. *And don't let Scorpio find my wallet.* My chest was tight and breaths shallow. *I won't do this anymore. I promise.*

I was finally able to catch my breath enough to climb into my car that was parked blocks away intentionally, and head home. But I was still scared.

TWENTY-THREE

What Doesn't Belong

SCORPIO

I knew my house so well that the smallest change stood out. Like tonight, the sensor lights looked brighter than usual and I could hear my dogs barking like crazy. It put me on edge even before I stepped out the car.

I cut the engine and sat for a minute. Spotted a shadow move from the kitchen to upstairs. It looked like Simone. My cellphone rang and when I looked at it, it was Raven's number. We just hung out, and she was sweating me already. *Not now.* I slid out slowly, gun already in my hand in case I had to pop some fool who probably thought he could jump out at me with surprise. I stepped out of the car, unlocked my front door so gently it barely clicked. The alarm didn't go off which meant it hadn't been reset. Either someone just left or was still here.

"Simone," I called into the dimness of the house at voice level. I ain't hear nothing, so I swept the house on the first level first. Then I saw it immediately. The back door was unlocked.

I crept out back, peeked around each shrub and trash can. The dogs strained toward the far corner of the yard, looking furious like they didn't get to finish what instinct started. Someone was here and I didn't need to see footprints to feel it, know what I'm saying? I glanced around as I walked the backyard, and when I happened to look up, I saw it. A colorful fabric caught near the fence line. The joint was torn. Stretched like somebody kept moving while it fought to stay. At first, I thought it might have been some neighbor's little shorty until I smelled it. CK One. I knew that spice cardamom scent was definitely a grown man, and I used to wear it. I folded what seemed like a piece of a shirt and tucked it into my back pocket, then headed back inside.

Every light in the house was on now, and it was too bright. Like guilt wanted witnesses and whatnot. Simone was standing by the kitchen island with her fingers locked around a glass of wine as she stood near the cake she baked. Like one of the two was gonna save her. The wine or the cake. She looked up too fast and smiled too late for me not to be suspicious.

"You're early," she said, too perkily in her satin robe. "Didn't hear you come in. I was in the shower."

I didn't answer.

"Where the kids?" I asked, just as my pager vibrated from my belt clip. I glanced at it. It was Rob's number. I'd call him back.

"With my homegirl, Stacey," she replied. "Spending the night. I told you."

She did, but that didn't relax me. I pulled the torn piece of the shirt from my back pocket like it was evidence. "What's this?"

Her eyes stretched wide. "I don't know. Where'd you get that?"

"Out back."

"Maybe the dogs got a hold of something."

"Or someone," I stared at her hard, stepped in closer. She blinked nervously. I grabbed her face. "You think I'm stupid, huh? DO YOU?"

She shuddered. "No."

"If I find out some other nigga was in my house, I'm gonna kill you and him!" I smooched her face, causing the glass of wine to slip from her hand and crash to the floor.

"Clean it up!" I shouted.

Just then, the house phone rang. I grabbed the cordless off the wall. "Hello?" I answered, irritated.

"Aye Slim, we got a problem," Rob said. I knew that tone. Besides, he never called me at home unless it was urgent.

"Spill it," I told him, turning my back to Simone. And right away he filled me in on the news, talking in Pig Latin in case the Feds was listening. He told me some soldiers got smoked. When you been in the game a while, you sense when it's coming. The streets was loud cuz product was low. Guys was losing patience since they wasn't eatin.

While Rob talked, I glanced over my shoulder to make sure Simone wasn't about to try no slick stuff, like hit me with a vase. She'd done that before, even stabbed me over a chick. We had our fights. Hard ones too. But when the kids came I tried to chill out. Lately, though, this disrespect was getting out of hand, know what I mean?

She was trying to play me and that pissed me off. No one plays me. I do the playing. And if it wasn't for my kids, I would kick her out right now based off my suspicion alone.

Plenty of nights I thought about Raven taking her place. She put it on me again tonight. After sex, we talked for a long time. She's a smart little shorty and come from money. She wants to be a news anchor or something like that. She doing big things and whatnot. Simone was just a couch potato with no ambition, dreams, or goals. Popping out babies and taking my money was all she was good for. But Raven? She that career woman type. Kind of woman that could help grow your money and not take it all. As Simone started cooking dinner or whatever, I could tell she was trying to smooth things over. Hide her sneaking, but I meant what I said.

"Yo, you still there?" Rob shouted, urgency in his pitch.

I popped out of my own thoughts. Replied in Pig Latin, but in English I said. "Huh? Yeah, yeah, I heard you, homey. Streets dry. I'll reach out to some cats back home in New York. Just call a meeting with the soldiers. Set it up for tomorrow. We need to get these lil niggas to make peace with each other before we end up in a bigger war on the streets."

"I'm on it."

We hung up.

I turned to Simone. "Don't bother cooking me nothing. I already ate plenty."

~

THE NEXT DAY

Raven's grandmother's house stood out from all the other row houses on the block. Not only did the crib look new, but the porch was lined with colorful flower boxes, and a rose bush sat in the middle of the yard. If anybody on the block had a green thumb contest, her grandmother would win that joint.

Raven was on the porch with her cousin Boogie, who was holding a cute baby in a yellow puff dress and headband. I walked up as the baby kicked her feet and sucked a pacifier, studying me with big ole eyes, gripping Boogie's finger like she could win in arm wrestling. She was cute enough to force the Hulk to smile.

"Yo, what's up?" I nodded. "You ready to go, Raven?"

She sucked teeth as she looked at her watch. Yeah, I was late, but I had some business to attend to.

"We won't make in time to City Place Mall, but we can catch the flick at Marlo Heights," I said.

"Seriously? You know that place is so ghetto," she complained.

"I got somewhere to be anyway, so if you want to cancel—"

"No way, we're definitely going. I heard *Above the Rim* was really good. If it's sold out, we can see *The Ink Well* instead," she suggested. "Be right back, going to freshen up and grab my purse."

Figured she wouldn't pass up the opportunity to be with me. I watched her slender hips sway side to side as she walked into the house. I shifted my gaze to the baby who started to cry a little.

"Ay yo son, whose baby is that?"

"Mine," he boasted with pride.

I thought he was frontin. "You mean your goddaughter, right?" I laughed.

"No, my biological daughter."

I always thought he was gay. Leaning against the porch rail, I caught a whiff of *CK One.* The same scent from last night. Boogie kept adjusting the baby. Either my presence was making him nervous, or he was just that into his baby cuz he kept avoiding eye contact with me. The baby tugged at his chain, and he gently freed her fingers. For a moment, I wondered—*CK One. Simone. Last night.* Was it just a coincidence? Boogie always been a loose-wrist cat, but now he's got a baby? Something felt off. Before I could put my finger on it, the door swung open.

I glanced up and saw Grandma Walker. At least, I assumed it was her. Raven always talked about her family, especially her grandmother. The sea green housedress and pink hair rollers made it pretty obvious she was the matriarch. Boogie handed her the baby, then wiped his forearm where she'd drooled. Grandma Walker said something to Boogie about it being time for the baby to eat or whatever, then turned her attention to me.

"And who are *you*?" she demanded, hand planted firmly on her hip with the baby rested comfortably in her other arm.

"Scorpio," I answered, twisting a toothpick around the side of my mouth.

"Mm-hmm. That a name or a warning label?"

I held back a laugh.

"Where you from?"

"He's from Harlem," Raven blurted out as she stepped outside, walked down the steps and entwined her arm with mine.

Grandma Walker squinted her eyes on me. "Why you come down here to my city making trouble?"

"No trouble, Ms. Walker, I'm just a businessman."

She snorted. "Well, you bets make it your business to have my granddaughter back here by a decent hour."

I chuckled at her boldness. She was lucky I respected my elders.

"Don't sweat it Grandma. I'll bring her home safe."

"Do that. Confidence come with receipts." She turned away, rolling her eyes. Walked inside with the baby and Boogie went in behind her.

Raven and I headed to the car. She squeezed my hand and smiled as she said, "Grams likes you."

"No, she don't."

TWENTY-FOUR

Truth Ticks Under This Roof

RAVEN

The moths drifted lazily around the porch light, their wings brushing the glow like they were keeping time to a rhythm only they could hear. I lingered there longer than necessary, humming a Whitney Houston ballad under my breath, my hand resting inside my Gucci bag until I slipped out the spare key.

I walked inside and flipped on the hallway light and climbed the stairs, slowing as generations of Walkers stared back at me from mismatched frames. From celebrations like wedding days and graduations, to simple and fun times like our family reunions. The Walker name always filled me with a particular kind of pride. Like, we were close in ways that didn't just seem polite the way it did with the Brooks family on Dad's side. Their traditions centered on golf victories and summers spent in Martha's Vineyard. Affection was… well… sort of implied through privilege and routine rather than presence. Totally not so with the Walkers, who were far more grounded if you asked me. I loved them. I loved my boyfriend too.

I smiled as I passed Grams's bedroom door. The sign hanging from the knob always made me smile: *I'm Not Old. I'm Seasoned and Well-Flavored.* Only her!

Leslie's room was right next to hers. It was Boogie's second home these days. With his parents, things had been tense, so Grams's house had become his refuge. Indy's crib sat against the wall across from the bed, pink blanket tucked neatly under her chin just so. Indy was nearly six months old and already running the place. Nobody ever seemed in a hurry to leave once they settled here at Grams, not adults, and not babies either.

Boogie was stretched across the bed with one sock missing. He was knocked out cold with an empty baby bottle in his hand. I leaned over him and whispered in his ear.

"Indy looks milk-drunk."

His big handsome eyes flashed open, blinking like he'd been yanked from a dream and forgotten he'd fallen asleep in his clothes.

"Mmm," he murmured, stretching. His shoulders stayed tight. "How was the movie?"

I slipped off my platforms, flopped down on a beanbag in the corner. "We didn't make it."

That did it. His brow arched slightly. "Oh?"

"Let's just say the night didn't end at Marlo Heights or any other theater."

He rubbed his face, thumb pressing into his jaw. "Figures."

"What's that supposed to mean?"

Instead of answering, he adjusted the pillow behind his head. Then adjusted it again.

His eyebrows wrinkled and eyes drew in like he was thinking really hard before he spoke again. "You ever notice," he said like he was measuring each word, "how Scorpio never takes you to his house?"

I watched him now. He wouldn't quite meet my eyes. His gaze fixed on the ceiling as if hoping to find the right words written there. The way he fiddled with the edge of the pillow gave him away. He was being cautious, not wanting to push too hard.

"No, I've never wondered that," I answered. "Dude, you've been acting weird. Every time I mention Scorpio, you get quiet. Like you're about to say something and then like, decide not to."

"I'm not acting weird."

"You are," I pressed gently. "The question is, why?"

Silence stretched between us. Indy grunted softly from our voices waking her.

"All the guys you dated showed you red flags you should be able to spot by now," Boogie said finally but in a lower tone.

I sat up straighter. "What are you implying?"

He closed his eyes like he was choosing his words from a pile he didn't want to touch.

"You don't know Scorpio the way you should. Just saying." He flipped his hands.

"I know him quite well, but you and Lucci don't see Scorpio how I do," I stated. "He's tough in the streets, but with me, he's so gentle. Being with him feels…safe."

"Safe?" He let out a dry chuckle. "Girl, I ought to slap a clue into your head. He's a drug kingpin, Rave, come on!"

I tilted my chin up. "Well, we all got flaws, right? Besides, I'm trying to get him to leave the game."

Boogie rubbed his temple. "Unbelievable."

"Why are you trippin?"

He hesitated, then looked at me so hard I could see his pupils dilating.

"Scorpio got a whole fiancée."

My chest tightened.

"And two kids."

I stood. "What did you just say?"

He didn't flinch. "Girl, you heard me. I'm right here."

"How do you know?"

His gaze flicked away. He scrubbed a hand over his face. "I just know."

"That's not an answer."

"It's the only one you're getting." His voice cracked, just slightly, before he locked it back down. "You either believe me or you don't."

I sank back into the beanbag, heart pounding. Too many moments rearranged themselves all at once in my head. Like the way his pager and phone went off constantly, followed by the rushed goodbyes, and every night he never stayed no matter how late it was. How many times had I mistaken his secrecy for devotion to streets?

The floor creaked, followed by Grams appearing in the doorway, squinting without her glasses.

"Everything alright in here?"

Boogie slid under the covers, pulling the blanket up.

"What time is it?" she asked.

"Midnight-ish," he mumbled. I didn't know if I should be angry with him, Scorpio, or myself after the bombshell he just dropped. Then I wondered if what he said was true.

"You made it home decent after all huh, Raven?" Grams asked, as she stepped in, peeped at Indy in her crib.

"Grams, I'm twenty years old. Why are you clocking me?" The hurt bled straight into my tone, and I'd never say 'clocking,' but I'd been picking up on Scorpio's slang.

Her face firmed. "Don't come in here like that. Just because you grown don't mean I should stop caring."

"Mm-hmm," Boogie muttered, eyes half-closed.

"I done heard things about that Scorpio," she continued, "and didn't know that was him until he showed up here on my porch steps today. The fact you made it back safe is a blessing."

"Here we go again," I sighed. "You too? I guess everybody hates Scorpio."

"He ain't no good," she said plainly. "You can do better, and you *deserve* better."

"But Grams—"

"*Shhhh…*"

Indy grunted like she was about to wake up from us adults talking. Grams reached inside and placed her pacifier back in her mouth.

"Your grandfather ran the streets once, too." Grams smiled as she watched Indy fall back to sleep easily. "He got into bootlegging and gambling and did a short stint in jail. I told him if he didn't come out changed, I wouldn't marry him. He changed. Got himself together and gave himself to the Lord."

"Maybe Scorpio will change too." I tried to sound certain, tried to make the hope in my chest sound less fragile than it felt. "People change all the time."

"That man in too deep," Grams said, shaking her head. "But you? You better walk away while you can."

Her words didn't land all at once. They settled slow, heavy, like dust covering something I wasn't ready to see.

"I know what he's doing isn't right," I admitted, my voice tightening. "But he loves me, Grams. I can tell."

She sighed, and it wasn't judgment, it was fear. "Only until you get in his way," she said softly. "And I refuse to bury another grandchild."

Bury another grandchild? She's comparing my love to the death of Champ?

"Grams..." My voice shook, as I stood. "How can you say that?"

She reached for me, but I stepped back first. "Raven, I'm not trying to hurt you, darling. I'm telling the truth. I've been on this Earth longer than you. I've seen how this story ends."

"That's your story," I whispered. "Not mine."

Silence stretched between us, thick and suffocating. I wanted her to take it back. I wanted her to say she was just being dramatic. Instead, she just looked at me the way people look at storms rolling in, knowing they can't stop what's coming.

"This conversation is over. I don't want to hear this anymore. Not from you. Not from Boogie or anyone else," I said, but it came out smaller than I intended.

My legs moved before my pride could stop them. I walked down the hall fast, holding my shoes in one hand and my purse in the other. I slipped into Aunt Irene's room, where I usually stayed the night, and shut the door harder than I meant to. But I felt torn between family and the man I loved.

I pressed my back against the door, cried a shallow breath and slid down until the floor caught me.

Only until you get in his way. The words circled me, but I loved Scorpio. Yet, love shouldn't feel like standing in the middle of a highway with headlights coming closer.

I don't know what to believe now or who to trust. Loving Scorpio doesn't feel like safety anymore. It feels like a countdown.

TWENTY-FIVE

Miles from Home

LUCCI

Tour life was fun as a mug. It felt like living inside a dope beat that never stopped. Slim, I'm talking about fancy hotels night after night, clubs, venues, and huge crowds screaming my name like it belonged to them. It was incredible! Can't lie, yo.

I iced myself out in chains, watches, studded diamonds in each ear that caught light before they caught sense. I bought a Bentley I barely touched. My closet was filled with clothes I only wore once. Everything was in New York in a house that Midtown Records rented for me. I only stayed there for business. As far as I was concerned, I wore home on my back. Like G-Ma said, my home was living out of my suitcase.

"...and tell your fans stop coming around here looking for you," G-Ma had said to me, frustrated behind the phone when we talked last. "My house ain't no meet-and-greet."

So, I upped security to keep the vultures back for a while and offered to buy her a new place. She wasn't having it.

"I'm not movin' nowhere," G-Ma declared. "Been here forty-plus years."

I could only laugh. My new fame kinda made the family famous too and gave them a more comfortable lifestyle. I took care of everyone. Starting with G-Ma. She didn't want a new house, but I bought her a brand-new Cadillac since her old whip kept breaking down.

"I don't need that," she'd protested, but I learned from her neighbor friend, Ms. Ann, that G-Ma couldn't stop smiling when they rode in it together to go play bingo. She made the other seniors' heads turn. Of course, I took care of Donovan's mom, Keisha. She flexin' in her Beamer throughout DC. I also gave her money to open her own hair salon, and I made sure Donovan was good, too.

As for Ling? She gets nada besides child support. I wouldn't spit on her if she caught fire. She had the nerve to come at me for ten G's a month for Lil Lucci. Straight trippin!

My lawyer laughed her right out of the mediation room when we met. "What is little Lucci eating? Gold-plated crackers?" he asked, laughing boisterously when he slammed his briefcase shut.

I countersued, and when she had to produce receipts, things didn't add up to make sense. The judge ended up giving me less money to have to pay for child support in the first place. So, for her to try to get more money, I now pay less. If she keeps trying these money tricks or whatever, my next move will be to get full custody.

Anyway, I'm backstage now. Just wrapped up another dope show before a sellout crowd at Atlanta's Philips Arena. I was the opening act for WuTang, Onyx, and the Geto Boys. Chopping it up with these rappers I once had on my wall was unbelievable, but I played it cool. We laughed over drinks, blunts, and talked smack. It was still hard to believe that a DC kid like me was even breathing the same air as these cats. They kicked some Hollywood game to me, and I soaked it up like a sponge.

In between the laughs, conversation, and just trying to chill and relax, Preston Silvers, my manager, whom everyone called "Chunky" hit me with the next move.

"Lucci, our next trip is overseas," he said, flipping through his calendar. Ignoring my convo with the guys, as he announced, "We're going to Europe, China, Japan, and Africa." He paced back and forth with his beer belly hanging over his belt and a cigar bobbing from the corner of his mouth over each word.

Africa stopped me cold. I stood up abruptly from my vanity chair. "Africa? I don't even think I have a passport."

Chunky walked over, reached inside his suit jacket pocket. "Now you do."

I flipped open the small navy-blue book and didn't even remember taking the passport photo I'd been so busy.

"Your ride is outside. Great show tonight. Tomorrow we're flying to Paris, so get some rest, huh, pal." Chunky patted my shoulder and dipped.

I showered and headed out, passing concert crews and band members with their instruments heading to the tour buses parked outside the arena. As I walked toward the exit down the long hallway, someone called my name, and I turned around.

Rah.

Same calm. Same eyes. Same energy that always felt like a deep breath. She walked toward me, bowlegged confident, heels clicking, and perfume greeting me before she reached up to hug me.

"Yu turned out dis place tonight, superstar." She squeezed me.

"Thanks, Rah," I cheesed all thirty-two teeth like I hit the lottery. "When you get down here to the A?"

"Yu not the only rapper needing a braider, mon. I'm a hair stylist. Me live 'ere now. Me braid for many artists at LaFace Records, SoSo Def, you name it. Atlanta treats me good." She smiled proudly, then paused, her eyes tracing over me. "But yu? Yu look tired."

I shrugged it off. "That's the job."

She didn't laugh.

"Come by me place when yu done," she said quickly, seeing the media headed my way along with fans who'd somehow found their way backstage.

She jotted down her address. I secured it in my pocket just as a crowd of fans rushed toward me for autographs. And Rah got lost in the crowd. I looked around and she was gone.

By the time I shook the last hand and flashed a smile for pictures, my legs were buckling from standing too long and my fingers were sore from signing autographs.

I finally made it outside. With so many artists getting picked up, drivers held up signs for the artist they were trying to retrieve. I saw a tall gentleman holding up a sign that said "Lucci Loot" and walked over. My legs felt heavy as the driver opened the door for me to climb into the back of the SUV.

"Yo, wassup, boss man, I need to go here." I handed him Rah's address.

"No problem. That address is College Park, I got you, boss. I'm TJ, by the way." He reached out. We shook hands before he closed the door behind me. Cameras still flashed everywhere. All I needed was a bed and some good sleep.

RAH'S GATE opened after I entered the key code. The driver pulled into a new single-home community. I went up, rang the doorbell, and saw movement behind the curtains. Rah answered, and I signaled TJ a thumbs-up that I was fine before he drove off.

"Come in, superstar." Rah blushed, stepping aside to let me in.

She was burning scented candles and something else that smelled relaxing. Tevin Campbell floated through the air low and smoothly. Inside felt warm, not temperature warm since it was spring, but warm like a welcome, ya feel me?

African art was spaced out nice on the walls, giving the space room to breathe and to be noticed. Tall vases with earth-tone feathers were placed neatly beside the living room sofa like they'd always been there like a staged display.

"Yu home now, superstar." Rah gently stroked the side of my face.

I kicked off my boots by the door. "Feels like it."

"Come." She took my hand and led me upstairs to the bathroom that was large enough to be a bedroom. When I walked in, the jacuzzi tub was already bubbling. I could feel the warm steam in the room, so it was hot and waiting with tea candles burning around the ledges. Rah slowly undressed me, pulling my Chris Webber, Washington Bullets jersey and T-shirt over my head, and carefully removed my chains. She didn't touch me like I was something used up, but like someone who needed to be cared for, and I was digging that.

Her eyes instantly blinked wide when she saw my package. *Yeah, girl. Any time you ready,* I thought to myself, winking.

She climbed in first, half-dressed in sexy lingerie, pointed for me to sit down in front of her. She wrapped her legs around me as she sponged my back, neck, and shoulders. It didn't take long before I was asleep in her arms like a baby. I don't know how long she let me stay that way, but before I knew it, we were in her bed.

That quick nap in the tub perked me up a little. We talked as our knees touched under the covers. About DC. About Jamaica. About how lonely it gets when everybody thinks they know you or wants something from you.

She laughed easily at my jokes and cried when I told her how hard I grew up.

"Yu sound like di songs ya rap."

"Because it's true. Some people lie in their music, but I can't be fake like that."

"Dats why me like you, mon." Her full lips curved a smile that made me blush.

"I like you too. Feels like I've known you all my life." I intertwined my fingers with hers.

She leaned her head on my shoulder. As much as I wanted to go further, for the first time, it felt like it wasn't necessary. The moment was special enough. Guess this is what folks call "intimacy" or whatever. We fell asleep peacefully in each other's arms.

The morning crept in too fast. I could feel the sun warming my face through the blinds. Rah had the house smelling like pancakes, eggs, and bacon. No woman ever cooked for me besides my G-Ma and aunties. My own mother never cooked for me. Not unless you count hotdogs or Oodles of Noodles or, as bourgeois folks say, "ramen."

My phone rang on the nightstand. When I answered it, it was a chick named Miko I was supposed to hook up with last night.

"You stood me up!" Miko shouted in my ear.

"Chill, girl, I'll make it up to you," I told, just as Rah walked in with breakfast on a tray. "Sorry. I'll call you later."

"Sorry? I wore my good dress and made reservations, and—"

"Gotta go." I quickly flipped the phone shut and turned to Rah. "Good morning."

"Is dat so? Humph!" She rolled her eyes. "You eat, den yu go."

"But Rah, hold up!" I grabbed her hand after she set the tray on the bed.

"Me don't share," she stated firmly. "When yu ready fi me, yu come back, so eat, den yu go."

I tried to joke and charm her, but she ain't laugh this time. She obviously overheard Miko. That boundary hit harder than jealousy ever could. She closed the bedroom door, and I could hear her trailing off downstairs.

Miko messed me up, and I don't even like her all like that. She one of them thirsty chicks.

While I ate breakfast, Chunky called to ask where I was. When I told him, he said he was sending TJ to scoop me up to take me to the airport, so I rushed through eating and got dressed. I didn't think we were leaving out the country so soon. *Dang. A brother can't get a minute to chill.*

Downstairs, Rah was cleaning up breakfast dishes, and I held her from behind.

"She don't mean nothing to me. You do."

Rah slowly turned around, looked up at me. "Dis was a mistake."

"Nah. We keep running into each other for a reason. We meant to be."

"Let me go." She tried to push me back.

I held her anyway. "You know you want me to hold you, Rah. Don't fake."

"Yu got too many women, mon."

"But only one matters." I leaned down, kissed her long and deep. She stopped just as it was getting good.

"Yu should go. 'Sides, dat yu ride outside." She nudged her head toward the window, and when I looked over my shoulder, I could see the black SUV in her driveway.

She walked me to the door. I thanked her for everything.

She stood on her tiptoes, gave me a quick peck on the lips. "Be safe, superstar."

"No doubt."

Within twenty minutes, we were at the airport. Chunky was there with my luggage. We checked in and then we were off on an international flight to Paris.

As the plane lifted into the air, I stared out the window, the city of Atlanta shrunk beneath me. For the first time, it wasn't just DC that I missed. It was a special feeling. And I knew that if I ever settled down and bought a house, I wanted Rah to be in it.

TWENTY-SIX

Home Is Where I Left Me

IRENE

I stood on the porch longer than I needed to, hovering near the door like it belonged to someone else. The house looked the same mostly, except for the new windows and fresh paint. I couldn't understand why I was so nervous. I felt more like a visitor making a house call than a person who lived here. Mama must've sensed my uneasiness as she fished out the key from her purse.

"You're home now, Irene. Let the past lay to rest. This here is a new beginning," she beamed.

The minute she unlocked the door, the smell of pot roast, collard greens, and something sweet baking hit me first. My mother's cooking hadn't changed. She probably got up first thing this morning to prepare everything. That steadiness settled me more than any grounding exercise my doctors taught me.

"There she is!" my sister-in-law, Naomi, shot a smile my way from the kitchen. She wiped her hands on a kitchen towel and rushed down the hall with her arms stretched wide to hug me. She held on longer than necessary. I let her because I probably needed it.

Henry stepped in next, walking out of the living room. He may have been watching some kind of sports game as usual. He leaned down and hugged me with his big, burly arms like I was a lost child who had been found. He and Naomi would visit me at the hospital once in a while. "Welcome home, Irene. Welcome home," Henry squeezed me.

Naomi had a warm expression as she stood beside Henry. I was happy to see the two of them still together after all these years. They were high school sweethearts, met at one of those blue light basement parties, and I knew they'd be together forever.

"Are you hungry? Come into the dining room and have a seat," Naomi offered. She was always pleasant and sweet. Teachers like her always knew how to make space without pressing too hard. I'd observed that about her over the years.

I followed them into the dining room where the table looked like a buffet of soul food. My nieces and nephews hugged me, including little Jasmine and Jared. Wow, they were growing fast. My mind tried to remember how old they were. Jasmine looked about eight and Jared maybe four or five?

"Hey sis, we haven't met officially, but it's nice meeting you. I'm Gerald, Diane's husband," he said, voice firm and deep. He was tall, brown-skinned, and gray-bearded. Almost reminded me of Henry, except he was slimmer in frame and looked like he had Diane by several years. *Sugar daddy*, I thought to myself. Diane probably saw dollar signs and ran toward him like a kid running to an ice cream truck, I bet.

Speaking of Diane, she was standing near the table, perfectly put together as always. Hair long, styled in loose curls that flowed past her shoulders. Makeup flawless, though she never needed much. Gerald stood back by her side after hugging me, rested his arm across her shoulder, while his free hand pulled Jared in. They looked like a family portrait on a brochure. A family I never got to have.

"Hi, Irene." Diane finally spoke, voice shaking a little like she was being careful. Like we were strangers who shared blood by accident.

"Hi," I answered politely because that's what I practiced in group therapy. Smile. Breathe. Don't let your thoughts wander.

Everyone still looked in awe when I spoke, especially Henry and Naomi, who hadn't heard me for themselves. A prayer was said and we began to eat.

Dinner was... awkward at first until Henry sparked the conversation. He brought up a funny story about a kid calling the police station because his parents wouldn't let him eat McDonald's. Everyone laughed, and before you knew it, plates clinked like a utensil symphony. Everyone started talking too loud and too fast, like they were afraid silence might crack something open. I focused on the texture of the tablecloth, the patterns and the feel of it to keep my mind from wandering. I told myself to stay present.

Diane laughed at something Gerald said, and jealousy slid into me before I could stop it. They were a loving couple, it seemed. A family with a routine. They talked about weekend plans, work, and summer vacation plans. I had *planned* for a life with Evan. *Evan Graham. Whatever happened to him?* I can't remember. I kept a polite grin because I loved being home and wanted everyone to feel comfortable being around me, but I thought of Evan often.

After dinner, I told Mama I wanted to take a shower and lie down. We went upstairs while Naomi and Diane wrapped leftovers and everyone else talked. Everything upstairs looked brand-new. New hardwood floors all throughout, windows, and doors, and freshly painted walls with family photos lined throughout the hallway as it was in the living room. My bedroom was still to the left and near the restroom, while Leslie's old room and Mama's were down the hall next to each other.

The door to my room no longer squeaked since it was new. When I pushed it open, immediately a floodgate of memories ran through my mind. I saw myself sitting by the window and children outside teasing me while I looked at them.

"It's okay. Whatever you're imagining, just know it's the past," Mama said gently, like she could sense something shifting inside of me as I stepped inside with caution.

The walls were soft bluish-gray with white crown molding, calm and breathing, not pressing in on me like the old beige walls that made me feel exhausted some days. I walked over and sat down slowly on the queen-size bed. It felt firm but sat low. The quilt was white with purple and lavender patterns. It felt thick enough to keep me warm on a cold night. The bedframe and headboard were made of wood the color of oatmeal. The old lamp with the crooked switch was gone, replaced by one that was new and lavender colored to match the bedspread. When I clicked the switch, it made the room look brighter. No more fumbling around to get it to light up.

I realized then that I was glad the old room was gone. Whatever happened to me didn't live here anymore. Still, the room felt quietly aware of me, as if it remembered who I was while I was still away figuring that out myself.

"Oh, Irene," Mama tapped her chin in thought, "I almost forgot to tell you that Leslie is graduating at the top of her class, and we're all invited to the ceremony in a few weeks."

I looked at her so fast my heart stumbled. "We're going to New York?"

"If it's okay with you?" She rubbed my arm as she sat down next to me. "We can take it slow, like the doctors said. If you don't want to go, that's fine."

"I wouldn't want to miss it for the world."

"Good. You can find the towels and washcloths in the linen closet in the hallway. I'll let you rest. You did so well. We're happy to have you back home," Mama kissed my cheek like I was a girl who'd come home after being away at school.

That night, lying in my own bed, listening to the house settle around me, I felt something close to happiness. The kind that tiptoes in and asks permission to stay. I was home. And for the first time in a long while, I wanted to see what came next, even if it scared me a little.

TWENTY-SEVEN

Between Shame and Survival

BOOGIE

Simone paged me, and I called her back from my home phone. We had been trying to figure out how I could get my wallet back for a couple of weeks now. She said Scorpio had some guys watching the house, and she was sure they would follow her every move.

"The guys just went to lunch or something. You should come through quick," she whispered as if her place was bugged.

"What about Scorpio?"

"He went to Lorton to visit Turk, but you need to hurry before his security gets back on duty."

"Okay, I'll do my best." I cradled Indy in my arms. She suddenly belted out one of those hungry cries as I hung up the phone.

Thankfully, I'd learned to keep my cash in my sock, separate from my wallet, after I'd been robbed a few times after leaving a party or club. Still, I needed it because of my driver's license and credit cards. Plus, I kept Indy's medical card inside.

After feeding Indy and quickly getting her dressed, I headed downstairs. Halfway down the steps, I could hear my father's voice and him mentioning my name like I was in trouble. It sounded like badges, sirens, and paperwork already filled out. Not loud, but firm, controlled, and measured. Like he'd already decided what I was guilty of.

My stomach clenched as I took slower steps, creeping the rest of the way down, not sure if I wanted to hear any of this crap today. Part of the reason I moved in with Grandma was to escape the arguing with my parents. They remarried after years of marital counseling and Dad getting sober for good. While they seemed happier, I wasn't. The two of them were always tag-teaming me about something. Either my friends or hanging out late like I was some kid. I would have lived on campus if not for Indy. Child, I just wanted them out of my freaking business.

When I reached the bottom step, I saw Mom sitting stiffly on the couch with her arms crossed. Dad paced the floor, still in his blue DC police uniform, boots thudding against Grandma's polished wood floors like he was mapping out a crime scene. Grandma sat on her famous recliner by the living room window, and her eyes looked worried instead of her usual jovial self.

"There he is. He's woke now," Dad said when he saw me, pointing like I'd stepped into a lineup. "Look at him, all rainbow bright and glittered. You got some explaining to do, Boy George Junior. Get over here. Right now."

"Last I checked, I was a grown man. Don't come in here with barking orders."

Mom spun on me, eyes blazing. "I beg your pardon. We are still your parents."

"Lower your voices," Grandma cut in. "There's a baby in this house. Boogie, hand her to me."

"That's another thing," Dad snapped. He stopped pacing and squared up to me as I handed off Indy to Grandma. "You need to start acting like a responsible father since you claim to be a man and stop embarrassing this family and yourself."

The word, *embarrassing* slid through my gut. *What was happening here?*

"You don't know what you're talking about." I tightened my jaw.

"Oh, we know plenty." Mom stood next to Dad and her voice

shook. "Here you had us thinking you were dressed up for job interviews, but you were out *doing* jobs. Do you have any idea how it looks to find out your son is sleeping with your pastor's mother?"

The room went dead silent. Even the air felt like it had stopped moving.

Grandma's eyebrows shot up. "The pastor's *mother?* I knew y'all said he was in trouble, but I wasn't expecting this."

"It's nobody's business, especially not yours," I retorted, looking Dad straight in the eyes.

He laughed. It was short, sharp, and empty. "None of my business? The whole church is talking about it. It circled back to us. You got folks looking at us sideways like we raised you wrong."

"I did what I had to do to take care of Indy, but I'm not doing that anymore."

Mom's face softened for like half a second. Then it hardened again. "Sleeping with older women for money is not 'doing what you have to do or should have done.'"

Dad's eyes stayed locked on mine. "I raised you better than this, son."

"No, you raised me to survive, and that is exactly what I was doing."

Mom sucked in a breath. "No, we raised you to have values."

"Well shoot, I thought Boogie liked bananas not cherries," Grandma said, earning a light laugh from me.

"I'm raising a baby on a college budget by myself," I shot back at everyone. "Who's helping me?"

Grandma rocked Indy, who had started crying from the raised voices. "I don't like all this arguing," she said evenly. "I've heard both sides, and now I'm gonna say my piece. Henry, Naomi, your son is drowning right in front of you, and nobody's thrown him a life jacket. I'm not saying what he did was right, but you shut him out the moment you found out about Indy. He never set out to get Nicki pregnant. But since he's been here, I've watched him bend over backward for this baby with a schoolbook in one hand and a bottle in the other. That ought to count for something."

Dad looked away first.

Mom wiped her eyes, angry tears slipping through as she said, "You could have come to us."

"Every time I tried, you made it clear that she was my responsibility. All you cared about was me going to school and getting my degree, but you don't understand the pressure I'm under."

Mom heaved a sigh as she paced the room, looking unsure of how to respond.

"Whatever that… situation is or was, you owe the pastor an apology. Today. Make it right so we can worship there again in peace," Dad interjected.

I nodded once. "Fine. I will, but don't think for one second I'm doing it to please the congregation and their gossip. God does the judging."

"Amen. And that's all that matters," Grandma muttered, rocking Indy.

Mom sank onto the couch, defeated. Dad exhaled slowly, like he'd lost control of a scene he thought he understood.

My pager vibrated against the clip on my belt. The number was Simone's again. I stared at the screen like it might bite me. I almost forgot I was supposed to have been on my way there.

Mom noticed immediately. "Who is that?"

"I gotta go," I mumbled under my breath, already stepping toward the hall.

Dad followed behind me. "After everything we just talked about, you're leaving?"

"I left something important. Gotta grab it. I'll be back."

Dad scoffed. "Unbelievable."

Before I stepped into my car, I heard Grandma yell out the living room window, "Boogie!"

I looked up.

"Be careful out there," she said just loud enough for me to hear. "Trouble don't always knock. Sometimes it calls."

I nodded and she turned from the window. Making me wonder if I was walking into another bad decision.

TWENTY-EIGHT

Caught Slipping

SCORPIO

I walked the narrow hallway like I owned the joint, even though the prison stripped you of that ownership illusion real fast. Lorton always smelled like old mops, sweat, and depression baked into concrete walls. Security searched me twice, hands rough, eyes daring me to flinch, but I didn't. A man who flinches in this joint don't survive out there. I knew. I'd been locked up before. It was a short stint for a marijuana possession as a young shorty, and I never would've gotten caught if I wasn't buggin out on it, know what I mean?

"Put him through!" the officer shouted.

The iron gates buzzed to let me in. I was escorted down the hall into a small room, where one of the cops stood in the corner like it was an interrogation room.

Turk sat behind an iron table in a folding chair, uncuffed, but all his power was still intact. His arms looked beefy like he'd been bench-pressing cars and whatnot. His skin was smooth shaven, but he looked mean enough, like he didn't need to raise his voice to be taken seriously. His dark, piercing eyes followed me down into the seat across the table. Eyes like most of the men in our family, including mine, except his looked colder. Like the kind you don't lie to, know what I'm saying?

"Hey, Cuz." I forced a grin.

"Hay yourself. Do you see any horses around this piece?" His tone was sharp as a blade. He leaned forward. "You ain't write and you ain't call me in months. I told you to check in."

Turk wasted no time to go in on me.

"Been taking care of business like you asked me to do, Cuz. Chill out."

"Whose business?" He cracked his knuckles, eyes flicked to the CO, then back to me. His voice dropped. "Raven?"

I felt it before I answered. That pull for a need to defend her. "Yeah, we been kicking it, but she don't interrupt business. She's smart, beautiful, and she's—"

"Family!" he shouted, hitting the table hard enough to make me jump. I hated that he saw me flinch. "She's practically family. I watched that girl grow up. And since you started messing with her, you been sloppy, man. A little birdie told me, deals been late or falling apart, it's been bad communication with you and your street soldiers, and dudes out there poppin each other and starting wars. Meanwhile, you supposed to be the HNIC, but you moving like your head still stuck between Raven's thighs."

"It's not because of her." I shook my head. "I got it under control."

"No, you don't." His eyebrows drew inward. "You're losing focus. And a distracted man is a dead man."

Heat crawled up my neck and brought fear with it.

"I know what I'm doing, Turk."

He leaned back, studied me like he was measuring a coffin. "You supposed to be taking the rein. Instead, you out there banging a chick who ain't built for this life."

"Raven's not our enemy, Cuz."

"You're right. She the *liability*. And you know it."

Silence pressed in. I felt twelve again. Like the little shorty who used to admire big Cuz. Then when I got old enough, he trusted me to handle things, but now I felt like if I said one more wrong word, he would make a call and have me erased.

"You don't need to cut her off reckless," Turk went on, pressing his hands together tight. "But you do need to end it quick before it ends you…or her."

That hit harder than his fist ever could.

I stared down at the table and tried to keep my hands from fidgeting. I could hear Raven's laugh, see her beautiful face lighting up from the good times we had together. I remembered her sweet smell and tender kisses. The way she looked at me was like I could be someone better than this B.S. She was special, but now I had to turn the heat off.

"I hear you," I said finally.

"Good," he nodded. "Get my lawyer another ten thousand for his retainer's fee by Monday. No delays. No excuses. I found some loopholes in my case, and if I don't want to be shipped out of here to Cali, we need to file it ASAP."

"I got you."

"Good. Just keep your head on a swivel," he warned.

"I will."

He held my gaze. "A man who's not focused gets caught slipping."

I stood when the guard tapped the glass, indicating that our time was up. I was glad. Getting scolded by big Cuz ain't feel good. I knew I had to pay Turk's lawyer, but ending things with Raven painlessly would be tough.

~

PRISON WAS STILL ON ME. That mildew smell was still in my nose and Turk's eyes was in my head. I couldn't shake the fear. He meant business. He sent plenty of dudes to an early dirt nap. As I drove back to DC while the radio played Northeast Groovers' "The Water," I felt like I was the one drowning and about to choke.

My phone rang and when I glanced down it was Raven. My stomach dropped, and I let it go to voicemail. I was already late trying to make a deal with an old connect with a dude named, Mike-Mike. Traffic had me hemmed up though. I tried to call Mike-Mike since he came down from New York to help us with our drought, but he ain't pick up the phone. I tried him again and again, and when he picked up finally, I told him to give me twenty minutes.

"No, my nigga, you need to be here in ten or I'm out." He hung up on me.

By the time I slid into the meet spot in DC, a back alley near a warehouse, it was empty. No Mike-Mike. No soldiers. Just a bunch of stray cats eating roadkill they'd dragged. I hollered loud at nothing nobody would understand, swung fists at the air like a madman. Then my phone rang, reminding me not to throw it. Maybe it's Mike-Mike.

Unknown number.

I tried to calm down when I answered. Play it cool. "Yeah, what's up!"

"You was supposed to pay me back my money today, are we still meeting up?" The voice on the other end asked.

"Who this, one of Mike-Mike's soldiers?" *I wasn't supposed to say that. What's wrong with me?*

"I don't know anyone named Mike-Mike, but I do know I don't like chasing grown men."

The more he talked, the more I realized who it was. *Tyson from Philly.* I forgot about him. I was supposed to set up a time to meet him today and pay him back from the bricks he loaned me. My hand gripped tighter around the phone. I coughed, tried to think of an excuse. "Oh uhm, I kinda ran into a delay."

A low laugh. "A delay?"

"Yeah man, but don't sweat it. I gotchu, homey."

"You got one week to pay me back my money. I'm only being nice 'cuz Turk your cousin, and we did business back in the day, but don't get that twisted. Courtesy don't get extended twice."

The line went dead.

I stared at the phone as if it was gonna explain itself. Truth was, I couldn't keep riding off Turk's namesake. I owed Tyson twenty-thousand dollars, now that's thirty thousand dollars altogether that I needed to come up with and fast. Ten Gs for Turk's lawyer and twenty to pay back Tyson. If I can catch up with Mike-Mike, I can settle everything.

Raven called again while I was trying to figure things out. I didn't answer. Instead, I hopped back in my ride and drove off fast. Dialed my top lieutenant and right-hand man, fifty-grand, Rob.

"Yo," he answered, TV playing in the background. It sounded like a basketball game.

"I need ten." I probably sounded as edgy as I felt. I was losing it.

Silence lingered for a few seconds.

"Scorp…" He heaved a long sigh. "You already know it's still dry out this mug. Everybody tight, slim. Why you think I'm in the house? Ain't nothing out there to move."

"How much you got?"

"Five. Maybe six if I win the bet on this game. Even that's stretching it."

Panic crept up my spine. "That ain't enough."

"Well shoot, it's all I got without sinking myself." Rob snickered. "Ling about to have my baby, you know that. Tried to get her to hit up Little Lucci father, and use that cash, but Slim done wised up, got him a new lawyer. So that's that."

"I'm scoopin' you up. Be ready. We need to game-plan urgently like a mug."

"Alright bet."

I hung up. Not caring about Lucci, Ling, babies, or nobody else's problems. Then my phone rang again. It was Raven's number.

I answered, feeling annoyed. "What you want, girl? You been blowin' up my phone all day."

"Well, hello to you too," she said in her usual Valley-girl preppy voice. I used to like it, but not right now.

"This ain't a good time."

"What's wrong with you?"

Everything.

"Look," I paused, but then decided to just spill it. "We need to cool out for a while, know what I'm sayin?"

"What do you mean, cool out?"

I stared straight ahead, waited for two kids on their bikes to ride across the street. "We need to chill. That's all."

"If this is about your fiancée, just tell her you don't love her anymore and that you love me."

How she know?

"What? I don't know what you talkin 'bout, girl."

"Look, I know, alright. Cut the crap." I could see her rolling her big pretty brown eyes behind the phone. "Clearly, if you're with me, then you can't be happy with her, right?"

A man who's not focused gets caught slipping. Turk's voice ran through my mind like a bold Post-it note reminder. I really didn't have time to play chess with Raven and Simone or to figure out how Raven knew. I had bigger fish to fry.

"Look, I can't think about that right now," I said, speeding through the red light, hurrying to get to Rob.

"I'm not worried about Simone. I was just calling to ask you to come with me to New York for my cousin Leslie's graduation. It will be totally awesome to finally meet your New York family."

For half a second, my heart fluttered at the thought of introducing her to my peeps, but I changed my mind just as I pulled up in front of Rob's house. He came out looking like he was ready for war. Face intent, black hoodie over his head, hands in his pocket, and probably holding a Nina. The only way for us to come out on top was for me to get focused.

"Are you still there?" Raven asked.

"Yeah, but listen, I'm not going to New York and you not meeting my family or none of that crap, are you buggin?" I answered fast, before Rob grabbed the door handle to step inside. "Time for you to do your own thing, shorty. It's quits."

"But Scorpio—"

I hit the *END* button to hang up.

I sat there with the phone dead in my hand, knowing I just cut something special that I didn't know how to fix.

Rob slid into the passenger seat, his jaw clenched and brows drawn together, a tightness around his eyes. "This gotta be bad, ain't it?" he asked.

"Worse."

We rode back toward my crib in Bowie and talked about how we could collect what little our soldiers on the blocks had without making them feel exploited. We knew if we squeezed too tight, they'd move on or we would become their targets.

As I turned onto my block, something tugged at me before my mind caught up. I spotted a red Toyota Corolla parked carelessly by the curb. The back end of the car was sticking out into the street and not aligned with the others, like whoever-it-was had been in a hurry. I slowed down at first and then drove past. Circled back slowly and parked in the shadow under a tree.

"Man, what are you doing?" Rob whispered.

"*Shhh*...just watch."

A door opened.

"Boogie?" I hissed. "You gotta be kidding me." He stepped out of *my* house wearing a rainbow tie-dye sleeveless shirt with bright yellow daisy duke shorts and matching yellow canvas shoes. He'd dyed his hair a brighter blonde and almost glowed in the afternoon sun.

"Look at the fag. Lookin' like he bought to join the circus," Rob laughed.

Simone followed Boogie to his car. She looked comfortable with him and kissed him like he belonged there. Something cold slid through me. Maybe it was Boogie's audacity or hers.

"Guess he swings both ways," Rob mentioned, watching the two of them as I was.

"Lil nigga bold too. He must've forgot who I am."

"Or he thinks you slipping," Rob withdrew his gun. "Let's remind him we not to be played with."

We watched Boogie walk toward his red car like he wasn't already in trouble. I pushed Rob's hand back, as I thought of Raven. "No guns this time, but we definitely gonna teach him a lesson."

We pulled up, and Boogie spotted us right away and tried to jump inside his car, but Rob hopped out, grabbed the door before Boogie could shut it good. Snatched Boogie up like a rag doll.

"Help—"

Rob quickly covered his mouth, shoved him in the back seat of my car. I sped away before anyone could see what was happening. Rob was in the back seat next to Boogie, squeezing his neck and calling him names.

"You got some nerve to be smashing my woman!" I shouted, glaring at Boogie in the rearview mirror.

"I...I didn't do anything."

"Sure you didn't." I hit the gas, sped down the highway.

We drove for half an hour, listening to Boogie belt out one excuse after another until we came up to the Bay Bridge. I hit the brakes.

Rob pulled Boogie out the backseat, despite his kicking, punching, and hollering like a little girl.

"Throw this lil fool in the water." I pointed to the river.

"NOOOO!" Boogie kicked and clawed wildly at Rob, but Rob muscled him to the guardrail and lifted him up.

"Please! Please! I beg you, don't do this," Boogie cried. "I didn't know she was your fiancée. I was just trying to feed my daughter. That's the only reason I charged Simone for one night of sex."

"Wait, Simone paid you for some sex? She's dumber than I thought. Desperate too." I couldn't help but laugh. I wanted to be mad, but wow. Simone was losing her marbles on this one.

Boogie cried so much he had snot rolling down his nose.

"Man, let him go," I half-laughed.

Rob turned him loose.

Seeing him bawl and wet his own shorts made me feel sorry for the dude. Just a lil bit, but then I thought about his disrespect and dismissed his tears.

"Don't ever come near Simone again!" I punched him in the gut, knocking the wind out of him, and then kicked him right where it hurts before throwing him into the backseat.

"You tell a soul what happened, especially Raven, and I will kill you next time. You hear me?" I sneered. He didn't answer fast enough. He was slumped across the back seat gasping for air. I grabbed his hands and bent his fingers back awkwardly. Even Rob squirmed from the way Boogie cried out in pain. "I said shut up," I punched him in the face. He squealed in pain.

I slammed the door shut. "Here, you drive us back." I tossed Rob the keys. I was so mad at Boogie and everything else I couldn't think straight.

Rob glanced over his shoulder. "He bleeding all over your seat."

"What?" I glanced back, pulled over. Got some rags out the trunk, tossed them at Boogie. "Clean yourself up, punk."

He sniffed. Wiped his bloody nose.

I didn't have time to play doctor. I was short thirty thousand dollars and time was the one bleeding out. Boogie could breathe for now. I think he got the message loud and clear, but there wasn't gonna be a next time. Word is bond.

TWENTY-NINE

Signals Across the Shore

MITCH

My mornings came with structure, whether I wanted them to or not. Years in the Navy had trained my body to wake up before my mind caught up. I moved through my condo on muscle memory alone. I walked bare feet on cool hardwood, shoulders squared out of habit, and spine straight even when no one was watching. Discipline had become second nature, but my feelings were not.

Chopper followed close behind, nails clicking softly, tail already wagging like his day held nothing but promise.

"Relax," I murmured. "Coffee first." I flipped the kitchen lights. The counters were clean along with the few dishes that sat on a rack. My space was still in order with everything where it was supposed to be. I reached into the cabinet without looking, already thinking about that first sip. The strong, bittersweet dark roasted bean flavor that opened everything within me and provided clarity before my day got complicated and busy. My hand stopped midair when I shifted a few dishes inside. Her mug sat right in front. Purple with a pink rim. The inscription, *Coffee is the best way to silence a journalist.* I felt my lips unconsciously curve into a smile. I bought it for Leslie last summer, on a day that wasn't marked on a calendar and deemed special. That was the thing about us, we made ordinary moments meaningful without trying. She laughed when I gave it to her, said it was too cheesy not to, and then used it the next morning. Of course, she then jetted out so fast I guess she…must've forgotten it.

I wrapped my fingers around the handle. The ceramic was cool, solid, and just as real as the moment I gave it to her.

Chopper nudged my leg, whining softly.

"Yeah," I lamented. "I know."

Chopper missed her, too. As I rested against the counter, memories of Leslie drifted back to me. The Navy has instilled in me a sense of resilience, but it hasn't taught me how to let go of longing. I finished CE school and had started a job on the ship as an electrical engineer. The job kept me busy as I continued my final year of Navy service. My dress blues hung in readiness inside my closet, serving as a symbol of perseverance. I couldn't wait to wear it upon completion. Still, Leslie's absence remains at the forefront of my thoughts. We didn't part ways because our love faded; rather, she chose celibacy, seeking intimacy that is lasting and sacred.

At the time, I told myself I couldn't handle it. That my desires were too physically strong and love would never adapt. After we split, there were other women. Easy connections with no expectations. I showed up, performed, and left. Just like the Navy had trained me to do. I was efficient, detached, and unaffected. Sex was like checking a box. And every time, it felt empty. Sex without love was just motion, noise, and heat without depth. With Leslie, intimacy had been more. It was meaningful, safe, and it was…real love. The way she'd rest her head on my chest like she trusted me with her whole heart. She let me be her first, and I never took that for granted. She shared herself with me and only me. Marriage used to sound like a restriction, but why is it I could only see Leslie in my future now, and the thought didn't feel hindered anymore, it felt free.

I poured the coffee and drank from her mug like it was a quiet admission. The bitterness settled my nerves. The warmth spread through my chest. Leslie was what I'd been missing. Not freedom.

Not options. Chopper dropped his head against my foot. He was ready for his morning walk, and I was almost ready too.

"Guess it's just us this morning again," I said, but even as the words left my mouth, I felt lonely, and it sounded false. Something was missing and had been missing for a while. There was no one else to talk to anymore or to laugh with. I couldn't even pretend there was.

I grabbed my phone and called Leslie before I could talk myself out of it.

It rang until voicemail.

"Hey, Les. It's me." I tried to use my same composed tone I used during briefings, but after hearing her voice, I felt a surge of excitement from her pleasant greeting. Decided to lose the cool-dude bravado and be real about it.

"I'm heading out for my morning run." I paused, held up her mug. "I've been thinking about you, and uhm…I wanted to hear your voice and how you've been doing. If you feel up to it, call me. Hope you're well. Bye."

I ended the call quickly and exhaled like I'd just broken formation.

Chopper was pacing by the door. I knew he had to go. I rushed to grab my kicks, and we hurried out the door before he made a puddle.

The day passed in a blur of jogging at the beach with Chopper, stopping at the farmer's market, the dry cleaners, and grabbing a beer and briefly chatting with the fellas. When I got home, my phone was blinking, indicating messages. I got so excited I didn't even put my groceries away. I dropped the bags at the counter and rushed over to the phone. Dialed my voicemail with lightning speed, put in my password.

"*You have four voicemail messages.*"

"Hi Honey, it's Mom. Just wanted to let you know that Bernard and I will be in Norfolk and we're wondering if we could pay you a visit? Hope you've got room for us. If not, we can stay at a hotel. Call me so we can chat about it."

Next message.

"Hi Mitch, it's Sara, we met last week at Billy's bar, and I wanted to invite you to a party I'm having tonight at—"

Message deleted. Next message.

"Hi Mitch, it's Jenny. Got something important to tell you and—"

Message deleted. Next message.

"Hi Mitch." Her voice echoed through the condo like it had optimistic powers. "It's Leslie, I'm doing well. Just getting back from my internship at *Seventeen* magazine. We interviewed Luke Perry, which was awesome to meet him and talk about the show, *90210*. Anyway, I'm home now. You can call me back whenever you get a chance. Bye."

I didn't hesitate. I called her back immediately.

"Hey," I said as soon as she picked up.

"Hey, yourself, stranger," she replied, carefully but smiling. I could hear it.

"I'm no Luke Perry, but I am glad you called me back."

That earned a laugh. "He was a really cool guy and made it easy for us to interview."

"I'm glad to hear that. So, does that mean you may start working at *Seventeen* after you graduate?"

"I love interning at *Seventeen* and I've gotten used to New York, but this pace is not for me."

Yes! She's not staying in New York, I mouthed behind the phone without her hearing me.

"You'll be completing four years of Navy service next year. That's awesome, right?"

"I'm still the same guy who forgets where he puts his keys."

She laughed. "Some things never change."

I laughed too, tension breaking.

Our nerves eased the more we talked. We were like old friends who found our rhythm We started laughing, reminiscing, slipping into old patterns like no time had passed at all. We talked so long the phone felt hot and I almost forgot to put away my groceries.

"I really missed you, Les." I paused in between dropping the ice cream into the freezer before it turned into a liquid.

"I missed you too," she said softly.

I smiled behind the phone. "I'd love to come to your graduation."

"I guess I have enough invitations, I don't know."

"Whatever, I'm coming anyway and none of them preppies will stop me."

She laughed. Just hearing her voice filled me with so much joy.

"Well, I better go shower and hit the hay," she said. "Tomorrow's another long day."

I didn't want to hang up, but I respected her time.

"Can I call you tomorrow?" I asked.

"You don't need to ask."

My heart warmed. "Have a good night."

"You do the same."

"And Les?"

"Yes?"

"It's good to hear your voice."

"Yours too," she said gently. "Good night, Mitch."

"Now it is."

When I hung up, I walked over to my CD tower, feeling a nostalgic moment from our childhood when Leslie and I lived across the street from each other. I pulled out Crowded House, played "Don't Dream It's Over." Because it wasn't over between Leslie and me, and I wasn't going to let things end. Not ever again.

THIRTY

Commencements and Connections

LESLIE

The warm sun rays bathed the crowd, casting a golden hue over the rows of spectators seated in folded black chairs outside the Low Memorial Library at Columbia University. My sky-blue cap and gown felt heavier than I expected, the fabric pressing against my shoulders as I gripped the edge of my seat. Pride and nerves made my stomach bubble as Dean announced the School of Journalism, beginning with the honor student's list alphabetically. As the Vs wrapped up and the Ws began, my heart rate sped up. With more than two hundred graduates and their families gathered, the crowd easily numbered over five hundred.

"Leslie Jolene Walker is receiving her Bachelor of Arts in Journalism. Ms. Walker, a Dean's List graduate, will pursue her master's at Howard University in Washington, DC. Congratulations, Leslie!"

Applause erupted. Somewhere in the distance, I heard my family cutting through the noise.

"GO LESLIE!"

I stepped onto the stage with my heart pounding. In that instant, all the challenges of four years living alone in New York without cousins, without my Walker family, all flashed through my mind. I had so many doubts, setbacks, and tough professors who told me to dig deeper with my writing. Yet here I was, graduating with honors. It had all been worth it.

The applause washed over me as I accepted my degree and shook the university president's hand. I nodded to the guest speakers squinting beneath the hot spring sun. It felt like crossing the finish line of a marathon I once doubted I'd complete.

When the ceremony ended, the class of 1994 erupted in joy. Caps flew into the air. Laughter and cheers shouted across the crowd. My family rushed toward me, wrapping me in hugs and congratulations that came too fast to absorb.

Mitch was there too, with his parents. We were friends again and lovers too. Starting over felt right, and even necessary. Maybe time apart had taught us how much we'd always meant to each other. Mitch had always been my best friend. I had loved him always, even when we had broken up. A part of me knew we would get back together. I prayed for us. Now look at God showing up!

As we hugged, I glanced over Mitch's shoulder and froze. *Mama?* She was walking toward me slowly, pride shining in her eyes. Tall, slim, hair blowing in the breeze. She was beautiful in her long summer dress and sandals. My mouth fell open. Mama was pretty. She favored Grandma in her younger days. Around me, my family followed my gaze, their expressions shifting, not in shock exactly, but relief. Like they'd been holding onto a secret I was only just being let in on.

Mama's struggles with mental illness had shaped my entire life. The noise around me faded as I stepped towards her, the crowd blurring until it felt like there were only the two of us. When our eyes met, something shifted. Grandma always said Mama's eyes were the windows to her soul. *Her eyes will tell you how she's feeling,* she used to say. Then, in what seemed impossible, I saw a light sparkling bright in Mama's eyes. Her mouth parted and time slowed as if the world itself had decided to listen.

"Congratulations, Leslie."

Her voice was smooth and sultry like a jazz singer easing into a note.

The woman I had known mostly through silent, subtle gestures and scribbled words on paper had spoken. The sound of her voice felt like a door unlocking somewhere deep inside my body, opening a place I hadn't known was still sealed.

Surprise gave way to gratitude. My hands trembled as I realized how rare this moment was.

"Your mom wanted us to keep her voice a secret, just for this moment," Grandma admitted. "She wanted to surprise you."

"Well, I am," I choked, wiping a tear. Mama pulled me into her arms and embraced me.

"I love you," Mama whispered in my ear. "And I'm very proud of you."

"Thank you, Mama. This moment means so much to me. I love you too."

I didn't know if she would keep speaking like this or if she was fixed, but her words were enough to make my heart feel full.

As the celebration swirled around us, I caught Raven standing just beyond the cluster of family, her hands folded in front of her. She removed her sunshades slowly, smiled when our eyes met, but it didn't quite hold, like it took effort to keep it planted on her face.

I recognized that forged grin immediately. The kind you give when you're happy for someone else, even though your own heart is still healing. She'd fallen hard for Scorpio, a guy far out of the spectrum from being her type, but honestly, I felt she was safe without him. I gave her a small nod. She pressed her lips together, blew me a kiss, then donned her shades to hide her pain.

I shifted my thoughts back to the moment that was big for me. Being a college graduate. Remembering how Grandma argued for me not to come here, slapped me for taking a stand for myself. We'd made up, sure, but it had taught me resilience. New York had tested me too, shaped me, and finally let me go, but what waited for me back home in DC was still unwritten. For now, I was off to celebrate with my family, and if I was being honest, I was "hungry as a mug" as Lucci would say. I wished he could've been here, but Chunky has him wrapping up an international tour.

THIRTY-ONE

Toasts and Tension

RAVEN

Sylvia's in Harlem was loud and filled with family. The air was thick with collard greens, ham, and baked bread. Mom and Gerald picked the place because it was known for its great food. The sound of plates clattering and laughter echoing off the brick walls felt almost exhausting, making me want to take a nap right there. I straightened my skirt and reminded myself to stay calm and focus on the moment. The Walker family had always thrived on noise, and tonight was no exception.

Leslie sat at the center of the long table, glowing at this moment and like, deservedly so. Her braids were styled fresh and neat, perfectly done and flowing past her shoulders. Her smile was easy and confident, like always. Everyone leaned toward her, replaying the ceremony, repeating her name like it was something sacred. I was proud of her, too. Hugged her and told her so when I saw a break in conversation. My cousin made so many sacrifices, and honestly, some I wouldn't have made, like turning down a good party to study. Insane! Pass me a drink, and let's dance.

Still, whenever someone brought up *the future*, I swear my shoulders got a little tense, like, okay, can we not?

The menus were passed around, all thick and shiny, and

honestly, I stared at mine way longer than I needed to. Everyone was ordering and chatting, but the chair next to me stayed empty. I set my Prada bag there. It would have been Scorpio's spot if he had actually come through, but heartbreak is rude like that.

We were digging into some seriously good soul food, honestly better than anything in the dining hall, when Boogie suddenly stood up and tapped his glass, all dramatic. I sat up straight, crossed my legs, tried to look casual, but my heart was beating way too fast and I had no clue why.

Then Mitch cleared his throat. Boogie dropped back into the seat next to me, grinning like he was in on some big secret. I mean, I've watched enough rom-coms to know what was about to happen.

"Guess he told you," I muttered to Boogie, trying to be slick.

"Girl, please. He knew I could keep it quiet." Boogie rolled his eyes at me, trying to play it cool.

"Whatever." I shrugged and flicked a curl over my shoulder. He's been a little extra lately; honestly, I have no idea what's up with him. Sure, he's always had that sarcastic vibe, but now it feels like something's bubbling under the surface. *Guess I'll deal with him later.*

Mitch stood, adjusted his suit jacket like he was stalling for time. He and Leslie sat across from us. His smile wavered nervously at first and then straightened with determination. Leslie turned toward him, brows lifting in mild confusion, her smile still easy and unsuspecting. Mitch cleared his throat.

"I wasn't planning on doing this tonight," he said with a soft laugh, "but today felt too big to let this moment pass."

I folded my hands in my lap and crossed my ankles, keeping my posture perfect, and my expression pleasant. If anyone glanced at me, they'd see exactly what I intended them to see: a supportive cousin totally glowing with secondhand joy.

Mitch talked about their years of friendship growing into love. About timing and growth and finding his way back to the person who had always felt like home. His words drifted across the dinner table, sweet and intentional, landing precisely where they were meant to.

Leslie's eyes began to shine, not with tears yet, but with realization. Her hand flew to her chest, a soft, surprised laugh escaping her lips when Mitch reached into his pocket, pulled out a velvet box. The ring caught the light as he knelt. Someone gasped. Someone whispered, *oh my God*. Plates were instantly forgotten, and time tilted.

"Leslie Walker, it would be my honor if you would be my wife. Will you marry me?"

Leslie's lips trembled. "Yes."

"Aww," everyone sighed, but like, in a good way.

Mitch slid the ring on carefully, pausing to adjust it slightly when it didn't glide the way it was supposed to. It fit, but it was snug. Just enough to notice. Leslie laughed through her tears, flexing her fingers once before nodding like it was nothing. I noticed.

We'll have to go to the gym, I thought automatically, already planning it out in my head. *Nothing crazy. Just a few sessions a week. She'll want her dress to fit perfectly.*

Applause erupted. Chairs scraped back. Everyone stood, including me.

Leslie glanced at her hand again, turning it slightly so the light hit just right. She looked radiant. Exactly as she should. She looked at me for just a second. Our eyes met across the table. Funny how Mitch used to be my childhood crush. He was still handsome with a boyish, smooth face and charm. I gave her a small encouraging nod. She beamed and turned back to Mitch, already lost in her moment, and I smoothed my skirt again, reminding myself that this wasn't my night. It was Leslie's moment, not mine. Still, I sat back down after we toasted and said all the right congratulations.

Like, honestly? Maybe if things with Scorpio hadn't blown up, this could have been me up there, or even with Dawson if life had worked out differently. But nope—not even close. And ugh, it actually kind of stung.

I put on my best supportive-cousin face, smiled so hard my cheeks hurt, and fought every single jealous thought as I got up to hug them both. I mean, who doesn't want that kind of fairy-tale love? The kind where your best friend turns into your soulmate and everything just clicks. Not the one where basketball always comes first, or where he's sneaking around with cheerleaders, or—hello!—

already has a fiancée and kids you know nothing about. How did I miss all those red flags? Maybe it was my own fault for wearing blinders. I never asked those dealbreaker questions Cosmo says a girl should ask before getting serious. So… yeah. *Ouch.*

I reached for my Nokia phone without even realizing I was doing it. Scorpio's number sat right there as a missed call, like it had been waiting for me to slip. I could step out and call him back. I missed his low and firm voice. The dangerous way that still turned me on, but I didn't move. I powered it off and slid it back into my purse before I could figure out how to talk myself out of something reckless. Or maybe back into something intoxicating and comforting. It was hard to tell anymore.

Someone further down the table shouted, "Cheers to Les and Mitch!"

I stayed present and supportive. I stood up like everyone else and clinked glasses despite being a little bruised. I smiled back, lifted my glass, and stayed where I was.

PART III
Why Did This Happen?

THIRTY-TWO

Queens Drama

BOOGIE

"And the real problem is not just your long solo act," Colors complained, poking out his lips so far that he looked like he was auditioning for *Duck Tales*.

Now mind you, we had just danced from Dupont Circle all the way to Rock Creek Park, sweating, dipping, twirling, and voguing our way through Gay Pride Day like our bodies were sponsored. And honey, my thighs were burning and my feet were screaming! I was *done*.

"What else you got beef with?" I looked him up and down, pausing my walk to guzzle down a bottled water from a vendor. It was June, hot and humid, and Colors picked the wrong day to fight. After Scorpio and Rob almost tried to kill me, I was exhausted from taking people's disrespect and abuse.

"You show up when you feel like it," Colors went on, rainbow hair glowing like Cyndi Lauper. "You miss rehearsals, and you pick and choose when you want to perform with us. We didn't even know you'd be here today."

"Because it's Pride," I retorted. "I don't need a calendar invite to be gay in public."

"Well, do you need one to admit it in private?"

"You know what. I'm done with this act." I flipped my hands. "You've been jealous of me since Hine Junior High School, and I don't have to take this no more. Should've quit this act a long time ago."

I yanked the printed bright orange Rhythm Rock Boys T-shirt over my head, sweat-soaked, and tossed it straight into a trash can without even hitting the rim. *Champ would've been proud I made the shot.*

"Well, honey," Spring Water chimed in, "we're not the only act you need to quit."

Spring was six-foot-something with a sunflower tucked in his thick hair. He danced like the tides were rolling in and had a voice like the drag queen movie star Divine after a nap and a cigarette.

"Why y'all ganging up on Boogie?" Flava jumped in.

Bless his fiery little heart. We stopped dead in the middle of the street while Pride kept marching around us. Queers sashaying past us in glitter sticking to sweat, whistles blowing, giant bubbles in the air, and somebody singing Donna Summer off-key but with feeling.

"You two are birds of a feather." Colors pointed at Flava and me. "Neither of you got business at Pride when you poke women for money."

Jealousy was dripping off him thicker than my sweat. I wanted to slap him.

"Mind your business, wench," Flava snapped. "If you didn't tuck yours between your legs, then maybe it would still work."

"Slut!" Colors poked out his tongue.

"Yo mama." Flava shoved him.

Next thing I knew, arms windmilled like two malfunctioning ceiling fans. Fists flew through nothing but humidity. They were close enough to smell each other's lip gloss but somehow couldn't land a single punch. Colors swung so hard he spun himself halfway around. Flava ducked punches that weren't even aimed right. At one point they both paused, blinked, then resumed flailing like off-brand Power Rangers rehearsing a fight scene. Child, it was the most comical thing I'd ever seen.

"OK girls, that's enough," Spring said calmly, stepping between them like a queer wizard with a staff. "We are not fighting today."

Colors blurted out. "Fine! I'm done with these two imposters. I'd rather have friends who know who they are than these jerks straddling the fence."

That one hit a nerve. I felt it right in my sternum and immediately stopped laughing.

"Let's calm down," Spring reffed. "Now Boogie and Flava, y'all might not like it, but Colors is right. We've been rehearsing while you two just freestyle life. You want out the group? Say it."

I clucked my teeth. "I just did."

"Fine," Spring tightened his mouth. "But one more thing."

"What's up?" I propped my hands on my hips.

"Y'all better be careful," Spring warned. "Playing games with women. Dressing one way tonight, another tomorrow. That kinda stuff gets people hurt."

"Whatever," Flava rolled his eyes. "Come on, Boogie. We don't have time for Rocky and Bullwinkle's shenanigans."

"Fine!" Spring yelled after us. "Don't say I didn't warn you!"

Flava and I walked a few blocks to where he'd parked his scooter. I hopped on the back. He drove shirtless, wearing a bright neon green bandana tied just so, and orange booty shorts clinging to his thick, muscular thighs that looked personally sculpted by a potter. Women loved him. Men loved him. He could blend and bend.

"Thanks for the ride," I said when he dropped me at Grandma's.

"Anytime, Boog," he nodded. "Say, what are you up to tonight, honey?"

"About to hit this shower and go pick up Indy from Nicki. It's summer, so we rotate weeks instead of weekends."

"You get my message about that old lady in Georgetown?"

"I did, but honey, I'll pass." I shook my head. "Think I'll take Keisha up on her offer to do hair in her new shop part-time."

He chuckled. "Spring Water got you scared?"

"No, but every time I look at my baby girl I feel fake and dirty," I admitted. "Colors may be annoying, but he wasn't wrong. Think I need to figure out who I am, and that's not the way to go about it anymore."

Flava snickered. "Well, more clients for me. By the end of summer, I'll have enough money for my college tuition and a car."

Before I could say more, he revved the scooter. "See you later, Boogie baby."

He sped off laughing, money on his mind and freedom in his wake. Something deep in my gut whispered that was probably the last time I'd see him. I watched until he disappeared into the distance.

"Hey Cuz, how was Pride Day?"

Raven was standing in the doorway of Grandma's house.

"It was the same as it always is." I sneered, walked right by her, paying her no never mind.

"Well, I was just…wondering…"

"Then, like, keep wondering." I mocked her voice.

"Boogie, what's wrong with you?" She grabbed my arm, pulled me back.

"Girl, don't touch me. Don't matter if I tell you. You would still do what you want."

"But I don't understand."

"You won't until it's too late." I walked on upstairs to my room.

THIRTY-THREE

Before I Let You Go

RAVEN

Autumn had arrived thankfully, and summer's ordeal was totally behind me. Now, I was only a month or so into my junior year and, frankly, it had been a yawn so far. My weekends were tragically dateless, my roommate was off somewhere, and everyone else seemed entangled in their own pathetic romances. Honestly, the constant talk of Leslie and Mitch's wedding was exhausting. Everyone had a boyfriend now except me. Even Tierra and Camille had disappeared into their "Boo-Things." We rarely talked the way we used to lately.

Blackstreet's "Before I Let You Go" played quietly as I struggled with loneliness and my broadcast class rewrite. Professor Parker called my news report script sophisticated but unengaging. I tossed my third typed script in the trash and decided to call Scorpio despite promising Leslie I would never cave. Good thing I didn't promise myself that, so I invited him to come see me, even though it was getting late. I slipped the Resident Hall Coordinator a few bucks not to say anything and loaned her one of my designer bags that she liked.

I showered, primped, and got myself completely glammed up. The second I cracked open my dorm room door; I nearly lost my breath. I hadn't seen him since we broke up. He leaned his tall body against the door frame like he already owned the room. But it was his eyes I always loved. Those deep, dark, and intense eyes that had me caught before anything else. The air between us thickened instantly, pulling me to him with a force I couldn't resist. He must've felt the intensity too. He reacted by quickly stepping inside, kicked the door shut with his foot, and pulled me into his arms. Kissed me without permission. Without a hello or how've you been. He got right to it.

The moment his hands lifted me and pressed me against the wall, I kicked off my spiked heels as every nerve in my body ignited. His presence took over me and all the space in my room. It was commanding, confident, and unapologetic. One swift move, and he carried me over to the bed, pants already halfway down. He moved like he knew the map of me by heart. Like when to be rough. When to pause just long enough to make me ache for more. A tug of my hair here and a spank there. Mouth-to-mouth, breath-to-breath, and fingers digging into his lower back. I didn't want to let go even as I heard Boogie's voice: *he's engaged with two kids.* He may have been Simone's mess, but he was my fix tonight. He had that gift of unwrapping me.

When it was over, I felt dazed and drunk in love all over again. We lay tangled together, hearts pounding louder than the soft music playing from the mini stereo on my dresser. My body felt emptied of strength, knees useless and limbs heavy. I couldn't move and didn't want him to, either. But just as I got comfortable in the fold of his arm, I felt my head plop against the pillow.

"Please stay," I whispered, reaching out for him.

"Can't." He slipped out of bed, his chain with the scorpion pendant swaying with each movement as he put his clothes back on. He got dressed so fast, as if he hadn't just wrecked me moments ago and wasn't headed to trouble.

He glanced over his shoulder as he tied his shoes. "You already know what time it is, shorty." That New York accent still heavy the way I liked.

"But you don't love Simone," I added, touching his back, trying to anchor him to stay.

He laughed softly. "You know what Tina Turner said."

"Then why stay with her?" I pleaded.

He paused like my question struck a nerve but then quickly dismissed it, heaving a sigh as he stood up and looked around.

"All of this…" His eyes traced the room. "This is who you are." He looked at the stack of books, my class schedule on the pin board, and photos of me with my Sorors at Howard's homecoming last year. "But it ain't me, B, know what I'm saying? We come from different worlds."

"You're smarter than the streets. If Simone can't see that, then she's just using you for the money." I eased out of bed, tucking the sheets around me like a toga. "You could be here with me if given a chance."

"I'm not a classroom type of cat." He checked his phone. "Look, I gotta go."

"I love you," I chased, as he opened the door.

He looked back at me with his eyebrows furrowed. "You buggin' out, girl. You don't love me, but you do love what I *do* to you."

My jaw dropped.

"Keep chasing your dreams, shorty. Some of us never had any."

And just like that, he was gone. Like he'd given me exactly what I called him for without giving me what I needed. The door clicked shut like the closure I'd have to finally accept.

THIRTY-FOUR

Targets Don't Sleep

SCORPIO

The night air was cool, so I zipped my leather jacket when I stepped off Howard's campus. Sweat clung to my neck, and my phone was vibrating again from the clip on my pants.

Unknown Caller.

"Yo," I answered, assuming it was Turk. He always found a way to call directly with his prison guard hookups. He'd been bugging me about paying his lawyer the other half of the $10k for months, but without a new connect, and the word traveling the streets that I don't pay back, I was out of options. Figured they'd just have to ship Turk to California. Things are so tight right now that me and Simone pulled the kids out of private school and put the house up for sale. I was operating off reserves until I could find a new connect.

"Hello?" A voice finally came in. It sounded muffled like they were covering the phone to disguise it. "Your time is up, Scorpio. You're a dead man in these streets."

The call ended.

I quickly looked over my shoulder, scouting the block of Sixth Street to see if a joker was calling me from a payphone so I could run up on him and handle business, but I didn't see anyone. The

Shaw neighborhood noise just rushed back in as I put my phone away and stepped into my car.

My phone vibrated again as I sped off, zooming through traffic like an '80s Frogger game, adrenaline pumping now. I checked mirrors in case somebody was following me. The phone vibrated non-stop, and I finally picked it up when I got out of DC and hit the highway. Got on Route 50 to head to Bowie.

"Talk," I answered, trying not to sound afraid of whomever was calling.

"Yo Scorp, you left me by myself tonight. What happened?"

Rob.

"I was trying to—"

"Trying what?" he flipped. "Man, them dudes was about to smoke me. You were supposed to be there and help with the deal. They thought I was the Feds when you ain't show up. Called me bluff since only you had the cash. If it wasn't for one of our soldiers who stepped in to have my back, I'd be dead. Where were you, man?"

I wiped sweat from my forehead. "Look, slim, I—"

"You went back to Raven, didn't you? Talkin about you had to handle business uptown right quick. You went to smash and left me in the cold. She messed all our money up and you let her. Man, I'm done."

"Rob, hold on," I said quick, hitting the brakes as I passed the highway patrol officers sitting on the side of the road. Couldn't afford to get pulled over. "I got it covered, son. Yo, all we gotta do is—"

"No, Scorp. Ain't no more *we*, homey!" His voice burned through the phone with so much intensity I knew he was ready to destroy somebody. I knew it all too well. I watched him handle guys for me, and now I knew he was ready to turn the tables.

"We ain't partners no more, we ain't boys, we ain't nothing. If you see me on the block, in the club, or wherever else, you bets look the other way or run while you got a chance. We done! That's on the strength!"

The line went dead.

I stared at the phone a moment, shocked at Rob's boldness, but a poor man who had his life threatened was a dangerous one. Now I'd just added another target to my back. Panic crawled up my spine. I lost my right-hand man. Never been a cat who got scared, but now I'm outnumbered. Once Rob put it out there for the young soldiers, the street corner boys, that I left him hanging, they'd come for me too. Them young cats ain't scared of nothing cuz they hungry and want to make a name for themselves. They take me out and automatically they get a crowned rep, know what I'm saying?

By the time I hit the house, it was dark, but in my mind, I was already packing. I flipped the lights and ran upstairs. Grabbed the suitcase and a duffel bag from the hallway closet and went straight to the bedroom. Clothes hit the bed in messy piles—no folding, no thinking. Just survival. I had to roll out and fast.

"Scorpio?" Simone called from the hallway, closing the kids' bedroom door. She likely put them to bed with a book as usual. "What's going on?"

She stood in the doorway in one of my New York Knicks T-shirts, hair wrapped in a scarf, eyes looking sleepy until she saw the suitcase and bag. Her face instantly crumpled.

"This is it?" She choked. "You're leaving me… for *Raven*?"

"Simone, listen—"

"No!" She flipped her hands to my face, tears already spilling. "Don't lie to me. I can smell her all over you again. You just keep running back to her, and she's ruining our lives, our business, and our relationship, can't you see that? We are broke because of her."

She grabbed my arm. "You got kids, Scorpio. A family to take care of. You brought us here from New York. We didn't ask for this. You can't just walk out and leave us."

My chest tightened. If I told her the truth, she would be more worried than she is now. I know my feelings for her are not the same anymore, but she's still the mother of my children. I couldn't put them in danger. If them street niggas wanted me, they could have me and me alone, but not my family.

"It's not about Raven." I snatched my arm back. Tossed more underwear and socks in the suitcase. "Just trust me on that."

She sneered. "Trust you when you smell like her? Trust you when you stole my engagement ring and sold it. Did you give the money to her?"

"What? No!" I couldn't believe she would think that. "Yes, I sold the ring because you stopped wearing it and I had to pay Turk's lawyer to at least get started on his case. Streets is dry. What do you want from me? I'm doing what I can."

"I don't want to hear that. You're smarter than to go broke like this. It's Raven. Rob was right. That girl Raven is the problem in this equation," she spat.

"Rob don't have no business telling you about Raven or nobody else."

"Well, that hoe got in everybody's way, so when I was worried about you, he fessed up."

I zipped the bag. LOUD.

"Rob's got his own family business he needs to worry about. Anyway, I'll be back when things cool off. If you sell the house, just keep the money for you and the kids."

She sank onto the bed, breaking apart right in front of me. "You don't know if you'll be back."

She was right. I didn't. But one thing for sure, this wasn't me choosing Raven. This was me choosing to live.

I kissed my kids goodbye, and got out of Dodge.

THIRTY-FIVE

Cousins & Confessions

LESLIE

Sunlight poured through the tall front windows of Bally's Total Fitness, as Reel 2 Real sang, "I Like to Move It" in a low volume that threaded through the gym. I watched between my own workout as people moved to their own rhythm with the clink of weights, treadmills, stationary bikes, or stretched their bodies like rubber bands on the floor mats. Everyone was moving like rivers of determination. As for me, I'd lost ten pounds since joining the gym with Raven. With twenty more pounds to go on a strict diet, I was determined to look good in my wedding dress in a few months.

"Girl," I said between breaths to Raven, "you gotta stop acting like squats personally offended you."

She wiped her neck with a towel. "It's called cardio. Suffer now, put in the effort, and look cute later."

I laughed and powered through the last few reps as I followed her guidance, looping wedding details and timelines in my head.

"Speaking of effort," I said, grabbing my water bottle, "Boogie has been a lifesaver."

Raven was doing sit-ups, or as she called them, crunches. "Oh yeah?"

"I think he should consider event planning. His ideas for my wedding are amazing. And did you see what he has planned for Indy's first birthday? And she's only turning one next month. He even figured out cheap ways to get it done. His creativity and vision are awesome."

"Yeah, I agree." Raven stood, started stretching her calves, while I moved onto the floor to do crunches next. "I'd tell him so, but he's still mad at me."

"Mad at you for what?" I huffed as I curled forward.

She hesitated. "He finally admitted to me that Scorpio and Rob tried to throw him over the Bay bridge last summer."

My head snapped up. "Wait—what?"

"It happened when he unknowingly slept with Scorpio's fiancée," she added. "Or whoever she was to him."

"Scorpio was engaged? Boogie slept with his fiancée? You guys have lost your minds!"

"There goes the judgment," Raven muttered.

"It's not judgment. I just can't believe that he…and you…never mind," I shook my head at a loss for words.

She sighed. "It's over between us, anyway. Last week was closure."

I turned toward her as I gave up on crunches and started doing leg lifts. "Last week? You slept with Scorpio again after you said you'd leave him alone?"

She shrugged. "I just wanted that old thing back, you know? But I think I'm ready to move on for good now."

Before I could respond, a tall, muscular guy walked past us, slowing just enough to flash Raven a confident wink.

Raven followed him with her eyes and winked back.

I shook my head, amused in quiet awe. Even sweaty, hair pulled back, skin glowing, Raven drew attention without trying. She always had, but she needed to slow down a bit.

"You know," I said softly, "when we were kids, I always thought you were so beautiful, Cuz. You and Aunt Diane. I admired you both."

Raven looked genuinely surprised. She stepped onto the treadmill, and I sat down on the stationary bike next to it.

"Aw, that's really sweet of you to say, Les." She blushed just a little before quickly pressing buttons to start her run. "If only I could get a man who sees more than just my looks." Her voice shook as she ran.

"I think the right guy is out there," I said carefully, taking my time as I paddled. "But really, it's about you figuring out who *Raven* is first. And what she really wants. Do you even know?"

Her eyebrows wrinkled into a puzzled look. "I think I'll know when I see him. I do know he needs to be good in bed."

"Raven!" I snapped, laughing despite myself. "I'm talking about *you,* not a man or sex."

"I'm almost twenty-one in a few months," she shot back. "What do you expect?"

"Well, again this is not judgment, but why not make a man earn you? Don't just give it away."

"So, first you say I'm beautiful and now you're implying that I'm a freak?"

"No, Raven. Listen, that guy who walked by us and winked at you. Why did you wink back?"

"Because he winked at me. I was just being polite."

"That's just it. You don't have to respond to every guy who flirts with you or bed a guy because he happens to like you or be cute."

"You don't think I know that?" She wiped her face with a towel.

"Remember Aunt Naomi told us to make a guy wait four seasons before we became intimate with them?"

"Yeah, and she was totally nuts to think somebody would wait a whole year for sex."

"The point is," I said, stepping off the exercise bike, feeling like my legs were on fire. "She was trying to tell us to give a relationship a chance to grow a little. Get to know the person first. And I think for you, Rave, as much as you deserve to be loved and want to be loved, you have to stop jumping in with your legs up first. Give things time. You owe yourself that. You've got beauty and brains, so make a man earn you."

She nodded, tapped the treadmill to gradually slow down. "You sound like Grams, but I hear you. Fair enough."

I smiled. "I love you, Cuz. I really want what's best for you. You've been like a sister to me all my life. And you're going to make the best maid of honor."

She stopped running, caught her breath, and stepped off.

"Aw, don't make me cry, Les. I love you too." She wrapped her sweaty arms around me, squeezed as if she needed a hug. Held it a few seconds before she pulled back enough to look me in the eyes. "You're going to be a beautiful bride."

"Thanks to you for helping me slim down. And I know you're gonna beat my face like a beauty pageant queen when the day comes."

"You know it, girl!" she high-fived me.

Just then, Mitch walked over, fully dressed, workout done, but his face was still flushed from weightlifting. I'm so glad he visits me often from Norfolk, for date nights and to help with our wedding plans. He will be finished with his Navy service next summer.

"Uh-oh," he smirked. "Why does it feel like I just walked into a Lifetime movie moment?"

Raven and I laughed in unison.

"By the way, Lucci just called me," he mentioned. That got both our attention. "He's in town. Said his plane just landed at Dulles. He tried to call you guys, but I told him we're at the gym, and your phones are in the lockers. He wants all of us to go out with him tomorrow night for dinner and then maybe hit up a club before he leaves on Sunday for his last show in Africa—or was that Japan?" He tapped his chin in thought. "Either way, I agree with him. Let's go out and have some fun while I'm in town too."

"Sounds good to me." I needed a break from all the wedding planning, house hunting, and trying to find a job.

"Cool. Wear something sexy." Mitch leaned in, kissed me.

"Alright, you two." Raven slung the towel over her shoulder. "Les, let's shower and head out. I need to get my hair done. I'm not going anywhere tomorrow until I get fly."

She glanced at a muscular guy nearby. He was built like a wrestler and leaned down to sip water at the fountain.

"Umph, look at the buns on him." Raven arched her brow.

Lord, please help my man-crazy cousin.

THIRTY-SIX

Hair Spray

BOOGIE

Honey, when you walk into Blue Bubbles Salon and Spa, you feel the vibe instantly. The place is all soft blue, gold bubbles, and that glowing sign at the glass desk was real cute and welcoming. Sky blue walls, plush chairs, lemon water, and fresh fruit were all created and designed by Keisha. She made sure it's a sanctuary, especially for folks the world tends to ignore.

I'm proud of Keisha. She hired me as a shampoo boy, no license needed, and the ladies loved me. Child, the tips don't lie. Even Raven waited for me. "No thanks, I'll wait for Boogie to shampoo me," she told the shampoo girl. Can you blame her?

Raven settled into the bowl like she'd earned the right to rest her head in the curved marbled bowl that cradled her neck just so. I turned on the water, tested the temperature against my wrist like I'd known how to do all my life from doing all the women's hair in my family since I was ten years old. I always loved the feeling of a woman's hair running through my fingers. I had a thing for women with long hair, and long legs, pretty toes and nails. They were so freakin sexy to me.

"Alright," I said to Raven, "relax your shoulders, doll baby. I got you."

She inhaled deeply and exhaled to relax.

I worked the shampoo into her hair slowly and deliberately. This part always felt intimate, like care without conditions. Family care, so don't get it twisted. Any other client and I may have slipped her my number on the low.

"So," Raven began casually, like she wasn't about to drop a bomb I sensed was coming, "I deleted Scorpio's number from my phone and blocked him on my home phone with that new star-60."

I snorted. "Yeah, but you probably memorized it."

She laughed, a real loud Walker family laugh from the gut. "True, but I'm not going to use it. Trying to put it out of my head so I'll forget it."

I paused for just a second, then kept going, fingers massaging her scalp until I could feel the tension leaving. "Good for you."

"I've been thinking," she continued, eyes closed. "About all I allowed Scorpio to get away with. Not just with me, but with family. You and Lucci in particular. And I shouldn't have ever allowed him to come between us. We've always put family over everything. You know that."

"Yep." I nodded, unsure where she was going with this. "You were the first one who came up with that whole 'blood over water' thing."

She tilted her head slightly. "It was actually Champ who helped with that."

I thought about it, smirked. "You're right."

And I rinsed the shampoo out, watching the suds disappear down the drain before I added conditioner, smoothing it through with a comb gently since her hair was naturally fine.

"I think I apologized to you haphazard, so listen." She grabbed my wrist. I stopped combing as she opened her eyes to look directly at me. "I'm sorry I hurt you. You've been like my brother and not just my cousin."

"I know." I blinked back tears. "Don't do it today, honey. Can't be crying up in here."

"OK, so let's skip the subject now. Lucci's in town."

"And?"

"He wants all of us to go out before he leaves for his last international show. You know, a little dinner and then we hit the club. Me, you, Leslie, and Mitch too."

"Leslie? Not little Miss Hallelujah."

Raven laughed. "I'm sure she's only coming because Mitch wants to hang out, so are you joining us?"

I shrugged. "Girl, I don't know if I want to be around Lucci, or is it Lucci Loot?"

"Boogie, let it go."

My hands stilled this time. "He made a promise, and he didn't keep it."

"Yes." She closed her eyes again, enjoying the comb running through her hair before the final rinse. "But he also gave you money whenever you needed it, including when you were in a pinch to pay child support." She cracked one eye open. "Cut him some slack."

I scoffed. "Girl, look at you, trying to be a saint now. Maybe that breakup with Scorpio should've come sooner."

She laughed softly. "We're done talking about him. He's the past. I'm going to focus on school and family from now on."

"I second that." I rinsed out the conditioner. "Now let's get you over to the dryer. Would you like to have your feet massaged while your hair dries?"

"Is your masseuse cute?"

"I've never known you to like women, so you tell me."

"Whatever. Tell her I'd like a massage, please. Woman or man, my dogs hurt after that workout yesterday."

She sat up slowly, and I wrapped a towel around her head, tucking it just right, like muscle memory from another life, to keep water from dripping.

"Did you see Grandma and Aunt Irene's hair when they came yesterday?" I asked.

"I didn't."

"I washed them up good, and Keisha styled them. They looked so pretty. Ended up going to bingo together."

She waved her hand. "Get out! Well, kudos to them, but I don't know about getting fancy for a smoky bingo hall."

"For some seniors, it's like going to the club. The music, prizes, and sometimes they dance. You should go one day. I went once and it was cool."

"Wow, I never knew all of that. What if Grams meets one of those handsome senior men there? We would have a step-grandfather."

Boogie swirled his neck. "Oh no honey, we are not having that."

"I concur," she said, following me into the room where the hairdryers were blowing softly. Not loud like jets flying in the air. Clients under dryers read the latest magazines or sipped on a refreshing drink.

"Boogie, I'm proud of you," Raven said before I pulled the dryer hood over her head. She didn't have to say what she meant by it. I knew. I'm glad I'd turned over a new leaf too. This kind of job felt so much better. I could look at my daughter and not be swallowed by immoral guilt anymore. Whether I planned to keep doing this or something better, it was going to be what I loved. Not something dreadful out of desperation.

As for Lucci, Raven was right. We are family. Family comes over everything, including money and fame. But first, a conversation needs to be had between him and I, and soon.

THIRTY-SEVEN

What Still Comes with Me

LUCCI

The black limousine rolled through Cappers slowly, its sparkling rims and tires cracking asphalt like it knew better than to rush through here. Same stop signs with graffiti spray-painted over it, sagging porches, and each brown brick home with faded green canopies clustered together like Legos. I knew the walls inside the homes were still paper thin, I'd lived in one of them. Right near the corner of 4th Street.

We came up to the corner where I used to steal out the corner store. I recognized some old homies shooting dice right outside. To the far right of the corner was two ladies with long trench coats, holding up *Watchtower* and *Awake* magazines. I always liked their *Awake* magazines as a kid. And one time, a Jehovah's Witness lady bought me some food out that same store.

"You look hungry," she'd said. I was starving and hadn't eaten for almost two days, and my stomach was touching my back. She bought me a loaf of bread, bologna, and snacks. I punished that food right there on the corner. I'll never forget that day.

I rolled the tinted window down, smiled and waved at the homies and the Jehovah's who smiled and waved back but looked at each other like, *who was that?*

The driver continued down the street and as we approached my block. I told the driver to slow down. He glanced at me in the rearview. Chunky straightened beside him in the front passenger seat.

"Here?" Chunky asked, his eyebrows shooting up in nervous surprise. He was the only white guy in the car, clearly out of his element in neighborhoods like this. "You sure?" His cheeks flushed, a stark contrast to the rest of us.

I didn't answer. A young kid caught my attention as he stood on the corner. He looked no more than ten years old and wore a hoodie that looked too thin for the weather that was getting colder. His shoulders were hunched and his chin was tucked, like he'd learned early how to make himself smaller.

"Yeah, I'm sure." I shook my head. The boy's nose was turning red, and he kept wiping it with his sleeve like he was used to nobody handing him tissues. His sneakers were busted like a mug—soles half-detached, laces mismatched, toes bent up like question marks. I'd worn those shoes before. Not his exact pair, but that same life, you feel me? That same old, *I'll make it work* walk. Same pretending you weren't cold because cold ain't care either way.

"Yep," I said quietly. "Right here."

The limo eased to the curb. I stepped out. Before security could even move, the kid stepped forward, clutching a cardboard box with a ripped school fundraiser logo taped to the front. Chocolate bars knocked together inside.

"Sir," his voice sounded hopeful but practiced. "You want some candy? I'm tryna sell enough to buy me a Sega Genesis joint."

That hit me harder than it should've. Lil shorty didn't want no food, clothes, or new shoes. He wanted a Sega Genesis. Most people would look at him and see that he needed far more, but I saw something deeper. I knew he wanted a Sega Genesis so he could feel normal in this abnormal life. He wanted something fun to escape this poverty he faced every day. He wanted to let go and forget through Sonic the Hedgehog for a little while.

I crouched so we were eye level.

"How much?" I asked.

"Five dollars," he said fast before looking away. I knew he was lying about the price. One piece of candy was not five bucks, but he was probably trying to keep some of the cash for himself.

"How much for the whole box?"

He froze. Scratched his beady head. "The… whole box?"

"Yeah. All of it."

His eyes darted, lips moving quickly like he was counting in his head.

"Uh… forty."

I peeled bills off my stack and pressed them into his hand without even counting. Lil shorty was smart, and I liked that.

He stared at the money like it might vanish if he blinked.

"For real?" he gasped, mouth wide open.

"For real." Then I slid a little extra into his palm and folded his fingers closed.

"That's for getting your math right," I removed my dark shades. "And you can buy plenty of games after you win that Sega Genesis for selling me all the candy."

His eyes filled fast with wonder, then he squinted, head tilting. "Say, are you Lucci Loot? I thought that was you!" he shouted. "Thank you, Lucci Loot. Thank you so much!"

Down the block, kids spotted us and what was going on. They snapped to attention and came running. "That's Lucci Loot!"

They came running. Maybe six or seven of 'em with their candy boxes bouncing, voices loud, laughter breaking through the cold fall air. Security stepped forward with their arms wide.

"Easy!" they warned the kids.

"It's cool," I said. "Chill."

One kid tugged my jacket. Another shoved his box toward me. Someone else in the crowd admired my fresh Tims. They talked over each other, eyes shining like I was Santa Claus. I saw my old crew in them. Same chaos. Same joy when something good showed up unexpected in the hood.

"Y'all calm down. I'll buy all the candy from y'all today," I told them.

Money changed hands. Smiles broke loose. One boy hugged me

so tight I almost lost my balance. Security tensed still, but I waved him off.

"It's okay," I assured them. "They can hug me. They probably won't get another chance to see me again."

When I finally stepped back, I turned toward the house I used to live in near the corner of 4th and K Street. The kids followed behind me, whispering.

"Yeah," one said, pointing. "He used to live right there. My brother went to school with him."

"Yep, told y'all," another replied.

The house stared back at me. The windows were boarded up with bent pieces of wood like somebody had tried to break in. I looked up at the window that used to be my bedroom. The same one I used to sit in front of and talk about my dreams out loud while my mother was strung out or had left me alone for days if she was on a binge. I was dusty Lucci to everyone in Cappers. Theresa's unkempt knuckleheaded son who washed cars just to feed himself.

I didn't understand if it was regret or guilt that I was feeling, as the kids ran off to their homes to share the good news with their families that I had returned. Before I knew it, mamas and grandmothers came out to see for themselves. The kids pointed my way like I was proof that they could make it out the hood too. Some waved at me from their porches, others approached me for autographs and pics. A few bluntly asked for money. "Yeah, I remember your mother, Theresa. Let me hold twenty dollars."

I could only laugh, and hand out a little something to the ones who asked.

Chunky rolled the limo window down, cleared his throat, and tapped his watch.

"I gotta jet, y'all. Take care of yourselves," I walked away just before a small crowd began to form. Security opened the door, shoved some back, so I could climb inside untouched.

As the driver drove off, it all hit me hard. I blinked back tears not wanting security, the driver, or Chunky to see me cry. I made it. When people thought I wasn't gonna be nothing, I made it. This place raised me, shaped me, and tried to break me, but it didn't own me anymore. I didn't need to come back and stand in it to prove nothing. I'd carried it with me long enough. I done my time here.

A small tear slipped out anyway, but it wasn't because I was hurt or nothing like that. It was because I felt grateful. *I can't save everybody,* I thought. *But I can open some doors for kids like them.*

That's when I thought about starting a foundation. And through that foundation, I could build playgrounds, offer scholarships and mentorship, tutoring, whatever was needed. Through my foundation, I could set up recreation centers and clothing and food drives. The sky was the limit.

Cappers didn't need me to return in order to remember who I was. It needed me to reach back and help. And for the first time, leaving Cappers didn't feel like running or trying to escape. It felt like closure and new beginnings. And that was dope!

GRANDMA'S DOOR barely cracked before it flew all the way open. My key was still dangling from the lock when she snatched me into a hug so tight the chains on my neck clinked.

"Look at my baby!" G-Ma hollered, smelling like Bengay and the Virginia Slims she secretly smoked when she thought nobody was watching. She shook her head. "You're too skinny. They didn't feed you on tour. Get in this house and eat, boy."

I laughed, leaning into her shoulder. "I been eating good, G-Ma. I swear."

She pulled back, cupped my face with both hands, thumbs pressing into my cheeks like she was molding me back into something familiar. Her eyes scanned mine slow.

"Mmm. You look tired."

Before I could answer, she shuffled back toward the kitchen. The stove was already alive with something frying, something boiling, something sweet baking in the oven. It was Sunday. G-Ma cooked like company was coming, even when she wasn't sure who.

I hung up my jacket, kicked my Timbs off at the door, dragged my suitcases inside. Fame came fast, but this house stayed the same.

Chunky and the driver pulled off. I told 'em I was staying the weekend. Chunky wanted security to stay with me, but I waved them off. In this house, I was covered. G-Ma stayed prayed up with a different kind of protection.

I settled in easily, and within minutes, a plate slid in front of me like she was dealing cards. Fried pork chops, rice drowning in gravy and onions, greens cooked soft and seasoned enough to make you do a happy dance.

"Eat," she said. "We'll talk after."

One bite and my shoulders dropped without me realizing they'd been up all year. M*artin* TV show was playing in the living room as thoughts of the road pulled at me.

"Lucci," G-Ma said, sitting down across the table from me. "Why the long face?"

"Nothing," I muttered.

She waited.

"Been touring like crazy," I admitted. "Crowds screaming my name. I feel it, but… just not how I thought I would."

She nodded as if she understood.

"I told my driver to swing through Cappers," I mentioned. "Gave a kid some money. His nose was running, shoes busted, and…lil dude looked just like me."

She listened, sipping her tea.

"And then you opened the door," I added. "Smiling like I never left. That love right there—that's what I miss."

"That's the feeling of home." She watched me like I was still ten years old, scoffing the food down because I was starving. I thought about those kids on the corner and hoped at least one of them would make it out the way I did.

As I was deep in thought, the door opened, and Boogie walked in. We nodded a hello to each other, and then he stepped into the dining room.

"You got time to talk after you eat?" he asked, one hand on his little hip.

I shook my head. "We can do that."

THIRTY-EIGHT

Clubbin'

LESLIE

It was Saturday night, and Lucci treated all of us to dinner at Houston's in Georgetown. Houston's was the kind of place where money whispered instead of yelled. The lighting stayed low and amber, soft jazz played softly through the room, the clink of glasses blended with quiet conversations from people who looked like they belonged there. While sitting at the table, I remembered that Mama said she had something important to talk to me about tomorrow after church, so I made a mental note to get home at a reasonable hour, so I could actually make it to church in time. I wondered what she had to talk to me about.

Lucci introduced us to Rasheeda Reid whom he called, "Rah." He smiled in a way that made me think she was someone special to him. Rah was a beautiful young lady with smooth dark brown skin. She told us she was in DC for the weekend, shopping along M Street with her friend Tish, so the timing worked out perfectly.

"Pull up a seat, hey, they're with me," Lucci told the waitress, and she brought over two more chairs for the table so Rah and Tish could join us.

The way Lucci and Rah looked at each other said everything. There was an ease between their shared smiles and inside jokes. The kind of comfort that didn't need explaining. They stole bites from each other's plates without asking, like it was already a habit. Lucci had looked worn since coming home, but tonight he seemed rested and at peace. Seeing Rah added to his relaxation.

Boogie and Lucci were back to laughing, too. Joking loud enough to turn heads. Any tension seemed like a thing of the past. Raven smiled, but her laughter softened quicker than the rest. I sure hope Scorpio wasn't still lingering in her mind. She'd been complaining about needing a man. Just hope he's not the one she plans to return to again.

Over dinner, Lucci talked about new music he was writing, and how in every city or country he traveled to, someone was handing them their demo or cassette tapes with beats they wanted him to consider.

"Gonna call my next album *From Cappers to Skyscrapers* and donate part of the proceeds to the Sasha Bruce House," he said, referring to the group home for troubled youth.

After dinner, Lucci's driver came back to retrieve us in a limo. A couple of Georgetown students recognized him and rushed over for autographs. Even though his face looked like *not again,* he signed whatever they pushed toward him for signature, and as more students came running, once they realized it was him, security pushed him into the limo in the nick of time and the driver sped off down a side street, out of the infamous Georgetown traffic.

The driver dropped Rah and Tish near their car. Lucci leaned in, kissed Rah gently.

"Call me when yu get back, superstar," Rah batted her eyes.

"Soon as I get back into town," Lucci promised.

"Where to now, boss man?" the driver asked.

"Kilimanjaro," Lucci said.

THE MOMENT WE WALKED IN, the bass hit hard enough to rattle my chest. The music was loud, and the bass vibrated through my feet. Cigarette smoke hung thick under flashing lights. Girls wore cropped tops, big hoop earrings, Doc Martens or heels; guys rocked baggy bags with party shirts, and chains that swung when they moved.

I squeezed Mitch's hand. In all my time at Columbia, I'd gone out once to a Brooklyn house party where Das EFX played all night. This was different. Security escorted us upstairs to VIP.

Raven had convinced me to wear pointy heels, and my feet were already screaming. I dropped into a leather chair in the VIP area, feeling grateful to be off my feet.

A waitress approached and asked for our order. Lucci chose Cristal and hot wings for us. Mitch discretely tapped my leg as a famous boxer walked over and shook Lucci's hand before walking off. Mitch whispered that a well-known NBA player was sitting across from us on a sofa, surrounded by women. Their laughter mixed with the music. He looked up briefly and nodded toward Lucci to acknowledge him, but they paid us no never mind. Perhaps we were considered Lucci's entourage.

At some point between our conversation, drinks, and laughter, Boogie disappeared.

"Wait, where's Boog?" I looked around.

"Girl, they're playing his song. He may not come back up here," Raven replied, sipping the Cristal.

The DJ dropped "Another Night" by Real McCoy, and the dance floor downstairs exploded.

"Let's go see where the real action is," Mitch said, pulling me up. "It's getting too bourgeois up here. Let's go get a few dances in ourselves."

He was right. More celebrities came upstairs but did little dancing. They mostly mingled and drank and enjoyed being sucked up to by the waitresses.

Downstairs, the DJ moved from house to reggae, then to hip-hop. Biggie, Nas, and then the famous DC go-go sounds. By the fourth song, I was exhausted. Boogie wasn't.

A circle formed around him as he danced with amazing footwork as if James Brown had taught him. Each step on rhythm, quick spins, and shoulders snapping clean to the beat. He moved like the music lived inside him. When he dropped into a split at the end, the crowd went wild.

Even the DJ laughed. "Alright, alright, I see you, Boogie." He bobbed his head, then he decided to slow things down, gradually easing the tempo to a slower paced song.

I didn't realize it was past one in the morning until I glanced at my watch, but my body told me it was time for bed.

Mitch went upstairs to let Lucci know we were ready to go. I stayed downstairs with Raven and Boogie, watching bodies sway under the low lights to slow songs.

Boogie leaned in discreetly to Raven, but I could still hear him when he whispered. "I'm about to light this J."

Raven giggled like a kid. "Oh, perfect way to end the night. We'll meet you guys outside, Les."

I frowned. "Really, guys? Refer?"

Boogie smirked. "Nobody says refer, girl. It's bud, weed, or a J. Relax. We don't do this all the time, anyway."

I watched as he and Raven weaved through the slow-dancing crowd until they reached the exit.

Mitch returned. "Lucci said he will call his driver. He should be here in a few."

"Good."

"Where did Raven and Boogie go?"

"Outside to smoke."

Mitch chuckled.

I shook my head. "That's not funny. I just… hope they're careful."

"I'm sure they'll be fine. Come on, babe. This is my song. One last dance."

On Bended Knee by Boyz II Men floated through the club.

I sighed, but a small smile tugged at my lips. "Only for you."

Mitch pulled me close, and for a moment, the noise of the club faded as we swayed together under the dim lights. I closed my eyes, letting the music carry the night to a gentle ending.

THIRTY-NINE

Collateral Damage

RAVEN

The alley behind Kilimanjaro was narrow and damp. Building walls had graffiti all over it with one infamous Cool Disco Dan tag. The bass from inside thumped through the bricks, distant now, like the night was moving on without us. Boogie leaned against the wall beside me, laughing a little too loud as we passed the joint back and forth and gossiped about people.

"Okay, last puff," I inhaled. Waved it back to Boogie. Exhaled as I said, "I am *not* going back to Grams smelling like this. She will trip out, and you know it," I stuffed a piece of gum in my mouth to camouflage the herbal smell.

"Grandma may ask if we have some more bud," he joked.

I burst out laughing. "Can you imagine Grams high on weed?"

"BINGO!" he spun around laughing. "She'd trip out."

Headlights suddenly flooded the alley.

I winced, lifting a hand to see that it was a car a few feet away with the engine idling low.

"Who is that?" Boogie wondered.

"Maybe Lucci called us a ride," I assumed, feeling the high kick in.

Two shadows approached. One tall and the other short. The

closer they walked into the light, I could see it was a man and a woman.

I recognized the hard pimp of a walk. And when the man appeared under the nightlamp, I recognized him as Scorpio's friend. I'd met him a few times. Enough to notice the scars on his face and the way trouble always seemed to follow him. His face was harder now, jaw locked, eyes sharp with something ugly. The woman? I had no idea who she was as she stood next to him like he was her bodyguard.

"Hey, Rob," I said, keeping my tone light. "Didn't know you were here tonight."

He didn't answer.

Boogie shifted beside me, shoulders pulling in. I couldn't tell if he was cold or scared.

"Don't talk to me like we friends or something," Rob shouted. "You ruined everything."

I tilted my head. "I'm sorry, but what are you talking about?" I wasn't sure if I heard him right or if it was my high.

"Our money's gone. Deals went bad. We are broke! And Scorpio rolled out." He flipped off stuff I knew nothing about as he stepped in closer. "And it's because of you!"

He pointed. The smell of alcohol hit me when he leaned in.

"I honestly don't know what you're talking about." I backed up a step. "Like—at all."

"Of course she'd say that," the woman said. I stared at her. She wore a long leather trench coat as she folded her arms like she was watching a business deal go down.

"Simone?" Boogie's voice cracked. "What is this? What are you guys doing?"

The name stung me. *Simone? As in Scorpio's fiancée?*

I glanced at Boogie, remembering what he'd once told me, the mess he'd been dragged into with her. My gaze shifted back to her. A short chubby woman with green eyes, and too much hair weave and makeup. She didn't look like Scorpio's type at all.

"The way I see it"—Rob stepped in even closer to me—"you owe me. And you owe Simone too."

"I'm really confused." My voice shook. "I—I think you've got the wrong girl or something because—."

"Oh, I got the right girl," Rob sneered. "You come from money. So, you gonna take a ride with us to the nearest ATM and make a withdrawal. Make things right. Tonight!"

"Rob, you can't be serious."

"You heard him!" Simone snapped. "Now get in the car. Both of y'all."

Her voice made my skin prickle because she sounded too much like Scorpio the way I'd heard him boss people around. Like she'd studied him for years and knew how to move.

Boogie shook his head. "Nah, we're not doing that again."

His hands were shaking at his side. I knew he was thinking about the bridge. About the last time Rob almost killed him.

Rob sighed like we were wasting his time. In one quick motion, he reached into his coat. The gun appeared. That's when I knew he was serious.

"I'm done playing," Rob warned.

"I am too. I'm sick of being bullied!"

"BOOGIE—NO!" I shouted.

Boogie lunged before I could stop him, slamming into Rob and knocking the gun sideways. Everything exploded at once. Simone grabbed my arm as I tried to pull Boogie back. Her nails dug into my skin. Instinct kicked in, and I swung hard, catching her across the face. She swung back, hitting me so hard I saw stars sparkle before my eyes. I felt her tugging my hair as we stumbled against their car. I freed myself enough to let her have it! Swinging like a wild woman and connecting.

"HELP!" I screamed. "SOMEBODY HELP US!"

"Shut up!" Simone shouted, reaching for my throat, but I kneed her hard enough in the groin to make her back off. She doubled over to catch her breath.

I turned to Rob and Boogie, who were wrestling on the ground, trying to grab the gun that had skidded across the pavement. Boogie stood up to make a run to grab it. Rob grabbed his ankle and pulled, and Boogie tumbled to the ground. I attempted to pick up Boogie when my conscious told me to grab the gun instead.

Rob and I scrambled for it. But Rob was too strong, he shoved me so hard out of the way that I tripped and fell. That's when I felt arms wrap around me and squeeze to muscle me out of the way. I knew it was Simone and used a hard elbow to her gut and broke free, as Rob grabbed the gun and stood over Boogie.

My heart stopped. Champ's face flashed through my mind. I wasn't about to lose another cousin.

"NOOOO!" I shoved Rob's arm back. The gun fired. A shot ricocheted off a trash can, and shouts erupted near the club entrance as the bass of the music stopped.

"Somebody's shooting back there!"

We all lunged with our hands everywhere, bodies colliding. Simone yelled something about the cops coming and ran back to their car.

"Now you die!" Rob aimed at Boogie, still on the ground, blinking and trying to see. He held up his hands weakly.

"No, please don't shoot," he cried.

I told myself. *Family over everything* and reached for the gun.

POW.

POW.

POW.

The shots exploded.

Boogie's sobs were louder. He scrambled toward me, clutching my shoulders, trembling. I didn't want him to die. I did the best I could.

Rob and Simone sped off in the car as sirens approached.

"Raven! Raven! I'm so sorry!" Boogie cried.

My adrenaline was going so fast I didn't realize what had happened.

Boogie pointed at me, his eyes pulled back in shock.

"Raven, you're bleeding!"

That's when I felt it. The sharp, burning aches in my shoulder, stomach, and thigh. My legs started to wobble and lose balance. My hand went to my ribs, and warmth spread under my fingers.

"No… no, no, nooo," I gasped. Disbelief washed over me when suddenly my legs gave out.

"Stay with me, Raven, please, please!" Boogie crawled over to me.

My mind fluttered with a thousand memories. The sleepovers at my house and dancing to *Soul Train*. Our family reunions at Hains Point where we ate Grams's spicy pickles and mac 'n' tuna. The way Boogie and I played dress up in my mother's clothes and makeup. Late night conversations about boys with Leslie, and when we were kids arguing about who was the cutest guy in New Edition. Cheering for Lucci and Champ and Mitch when they played basketball against other neighborhood guys or football in the street. Family had always been my lifeblood.

"I… I love you…" I tried to whisper, my voice barely audible. My strength was slipping fast.

Boogie's arms clung tighter around me. "No, I'm not losing you too. I swear! Please stay!"

Even as terror threatened to swallow me whole, my vision flickered just a little longer to catch sight of my cousins' desperate faces appearing through the alleyway lights. Leslie, Lucci, and Mitch's voices were distant and muffled, like I was underwater, and they were shouting for me to stay anchored in the present. To fight. Something about help coming.

I hadn't chosen family over everything. I chose someone, a man who had torn our lives apart. I should've listened to Grams when she warned Scorpio was trouble. Now, as the world dimmed around me, I tried to open my mouth and tell my cousins one last time that I loved them before I couldn't, but everything around me began to fade too fast. And then… it all went silent…

To be continued…

Cousins 3: Family Always & Forever

The final book,
coming soon!

About the Author

Selena Haskins is a seasoned author whose character-driven storytelling reflects over a decade of dedication to her craft. Her diverse body of work spans multiple genres, including family sagas, romance, children's literature, and poetry. Recognized for her compelling voice, her work has been featured on NBC News 4 (Washington, DC) and continues to resonate with readers of all ages, especially young audiences. Known for creating emotionally rich characters and authentic, true-to-life narratives, Selena weaves faith-centered themes seamlessly into her storytelling.

Raised in Washington, DC, she draws inspiration from her life experiences, her community, and her deep-rooted commitment to faith, family, and purpose.

When she's not writing, Selena enjoys spending quality time with loved ones, traveling, watching basketball, or relaxing by the sea.

Discover more of Selena Haskins' inspiring stories by exploring her collection of books available now on Amazon.

Stay connected with Selena Haskins

Instagram
@booksbyselena

Facebook
Author Selena Haskins
and
@booksbyselena

Amazon
Author Selena Haskins

www.ingramcontent.com/pod-product-compliance
Lightning Source LLC
LaVergne TN
LVHW050624100826
845148LV00011B/1719

* 9 7 9 8 2 1 8 6 1 9 2 9 9 *